Burning Road

A Devil's Cartel MC novel

Book One

BY

SKYLA MADI

Burning Road

Limitless Publishing, LLC
Kailua, HI 96734
www.limitlesspublishing.com

Formatting: Limitless Publishing

ISBN-13: 978-1-64034-774-8
ISBN-10: 1-64034-774-7

THE DEVIL'S CARTEL
HEIRACHY

PRESIDENT
DAMON JUDGE
"JUDGE"

—

VICE PRESIDENT
JAMES CREED
"CREED"

—

ROAD CAPTAIN
SOREN REYES
"HAWK"

—

SARGEANT AT ARMS
KYLE WILLIAMS
"ARMI"

—

SECRETARY
JASON ROTH
"STOIC"

—

TREASURER
MATTHEW ROYAL
"CASINO"

—

PROPSECT 1
KACE RYAN

—

PROSPECT 2
IRIS SAITO

—

<u>NOTABLE PATCH MEMBERS</u>

SORA *"RAH"* KIMURA, AARON *"AYR"* ST. CROSS, FRANCES "MODO" MACINTYRE, CYRYS *"CY"* AHMADI, AMANI LEWIS, HARLEI HART, PEARL HART

—

<u>OLD LADIES</u>

NONE

TERMINOLOGY

1%ER (ONE PERCENTER): The term was coined when the AMA (American Motorcycle Association) was said to make a statement in response to the 1947 Hollister Riot that 99% of motorcycle riders are law-abiding citizens. The remaining one percent belonged to outlaw clubs/gangs who took the term and wore it proudly on their cuts, usually encompassed by a diamond shape.

43: The numerals that coincide with the alphabet letter "D" for Devil's and "C" for Cartel.

BITCH: Another word for "girlfriend," a term of endearment.

BRAIN BUCKET: A small beanie-like helmet not usually approved by the Department of Transport.

CAGE: A vehicle that isn't a motorcycle. For example, a car, truck, van, etc.

CABBAGE: Idiot.

COLORS: The club emblem/numbers/insignias.

CUT: Leather vest with club colors. Usually has no sleeves.

DCMC: Devil's Cartel Motorcycle Club.

DRAG BARS: Low, flat, and straight motorcycle handlebars.

FENDER FLUFF: A female passenger invited for a ride on the back of a motorcycle. Not an old lady.

FLYING LOW: Speeding.

MAMA: A woman who is willing to have sex with all members of the gang, usually at the same time (see "Pull a Train"). The term is only used for women who regularly associate with the club and entertain multiple members on a very regular basis.

NOMAD: An individual who isn't a member of a motorcycle group and isn't locked to a certain territory.

NORMIES: Civilians/townspeople.

OLD LADY: A wife or long-time girlfriend. It has nothing to do with age and is **_not_** a derogatory term.

PATCHWHORE: A female who has sex with members of a motorcycle club, solely members who have been patched into the club. No one has ownership over these women, and they can have sex with whoever they like. Other variations include: Patchrider, clubslut, and clubwhore.

PIG: A derogatory term for a police officer.

PULL A TRAIN: The act of having sex with multiple (if not ALL) of the members.

RUNNING 66: Riding without wearing club colors.

SMOKE: Cigarette

SNOW: Cocaine. Other variations include: Blow.

"Love has nothing to do with what you are expecting to get—
only with what you are expecting to give—which is everything."

—Katharine Hepburn

ONE

IZZY

The first time I met James Creed was in my bedroom one year ago. I smelled him before I saw him. Ambrosial wafts of leather, cologne, and burning rubber murdered the gentle fragrance of lavender in my private space, tainting everything with his manly scent. His boots sounded heavy, even against the carpet, and squeaked with stress as he walked further into my room. When he stopped, chains clashed together then fell silent as he cleared his throat. My lips parted. The sound of his approach was as beautiful as any Mozart piece, his presence a symphony that sang to my blood.

I peered out my bedroom window, staring at the terrifying motorcycle he pulled up on, following his friend. I hadn't seen his face, but I knew it was him. His shoulders were broad and his ass tight in his dark jeans. No one wore black denim, faded tees, and leather like he did.

I saw Creed around town a handful of times

1

before tonight. On a rare occasion, when my father loosened the reins, I'd go with friends to the outskirts of town, where the vicious underbelly of Exeter festered. It was off limits to me since my father, the mayor, vowed to clean it up.

I first made eye contact with James Creed outside a rundown convenience store across from a bar. He was sitting on his motorcycle as my friends and I sauntered by. His presence commanded my attention, and I powerlessly gave it. Creed raked me from head to toe with his whiskey-gold stare, turning my blood to lava, my skin to fireworks. As the mayor's daughter, I'd always dressed conservatively to avoid negative press. The day Creed noticed me, I wore an innocent and sophisticated honey-colored dress that sat an inch above my knees and a pair of matching flats. My long, blonde hair was pinned back, my soft waves well out of my face. Under his gaze, I felt naked, like I was wearing nothing but a leather thong and a studded collar. I was breathless, aroused, and enraptured. He made me feel all the things a seventeen-year-old girl had no business feeling, and I relished it. I was instantly attracted to him, to the fact he was the opposite of every other man in my life. I was used to elegant men who wore suits and pressed polos with crisp collars, men who were polished and refined. Creed was rugged and rough. His shirts were faded, the collars slightly stretched. His jeans were marked and his shoes scuffed. His tan skin was painted with stunning swirls of ink, his hair a tousled mess, and his face freshly shaven.

Creed of the Devil's Cartel MC was an alpha

male, a powerful embodiment of masculinity, and that day in the street outside the bar, when he gave me a small flick of his wrist and flashed me a killer smile, he had me hook, line, and sinker. I'd been infatuated with him ever since.

Three years later, he stood behind me in my bedroom, on the eve of my twenty-first birthday, stealing all the oxygen from my lungs. My heart pounded in my chest, slamming into my ribs with the force of a sledgehammer behind it. I knew my father was doing dodgy deals with the Devil's Cartel, but they had never brought it to the house before. Something was wrong.

Very wrong.

Somewhere in the house, my father yelped, and I jumped, gripping the window frame in my manicured hand. What had he got himself into this time? My father was an intelligent man but a tad ambitious. His campaign promise to make Exeter a safer place and lower gang-related crime was what got him elected. It put a target on his back, too. When he realized the roots of gang-related crime went deeper than what was shown on the surface, he had to improvise. He paid big criminals, like the Devil's Cartel, to be discreet with their crime, so he could pretend gang-related crime was on the decline. The people of the town thought it was safer now my father was in control of things. The people of the town were stupid.

"Are you…" I croaked, my voice a cracking mess.

I swallowed hard, but there was no saliva to moisten my tongue to better project the words I wanted to speak.

"If you've got something to say, Blondie, at least show me your pretty face."

I gritted my teeth at his gravelly voice. His deep tenor played my spine like a xylophone, sending ripples through my body with every syllable that fell from his lips. I pressed my hand to my bare, flat stomach. Since I was preparing to sleep, I was wearing nothing but a crop top and a pair of bed shorts much too short, much too revealing. I sucked in a breath and slowly turned around. I kept my stare downcast to my beige, pink-tinged shaggy rug.

His big boots rested on the edge of it, the harsh black leather creating disharmony with the light color scheme of my room. I hesitated to lift my attention to him. I knew what he looked like. I'd seen him in the light of day when the sun turned his hair from a cold black to warm, dark chocolate with ochre highlights. I'd seen sunlight bounce off his high cheekbones and smooth forehead, but still, I was terrified to see him in the dim light of my room. What if he was nothing like I'd built him up in my head?

"Mm," he hummed, amused. "Now grace me with those big, blue eyes of yours."

Blue? Surprised, I flicked my stare to his, and the corners of his lips twitched. He knew what color my eyes were? Creed stepped forward, and I tensed, straightening my spine and squaring my shoulders. He was as beautiful as I remembered with his golden eyes and dark hair that was short at the sides but long at the top. He had alluring full lips and smelled of whiskey and asphalt. I'd never smelled anything so lethal, so perfect. I flicked my gaze over his aged leather vest, over patches that clearly held meaning I didn't understand, and admired his tan skin, the perfect canvas to showcase his intricate ink. What was he doing here? In my room? Another shout from my father pierced the air, and I startled, my pulse pounding rapidly.

"Please don't hurt my dad," I pleaded, my lower lip trembling as I looked him in the eyes. "What do you want? Money?"

"Money? Nah." He turned away, something on my vanity catching his eye. "Got plenty of that."

I frowned and watched him closely as he reached out and touched the marble top, analyzing the contents that littered its surface—makeup, hair products, jewelry, and photos.

"So much fucking pink," he muttered, lifting a set of white and pink cheerleading pom-poms I hadn't used since high school.

The way he judged my personal items was humiliating. He plucked lip balms and decorated headbands and surveyed them with a quirk on his lips before setting them down again. Creed lowered his large hand to the handle of the first drawer, and I sucked air between my lips as fierce heat burned up my neck and settled in my cheeks. Creed eased the drawer open, exposing my collection of panties. Without a care, he plucked a baby pink pair off the top and lifted it, letting it hang from his fingers. His amusement made me feel like a child and pathetically inferior. Did his lovers wear black thongs instead of pink? Did they have genital piercings and naughty tattoos? In comparison, maybe I did look like a child to him.

I pursed my lips against the urge to demand he stop snooping because, tucked into his waistband, I caught a glimpse of his handgun, and ice crystalized in my veins.

"A-are you…" I swallowed hard, unable to take my eyes off his lower back, where his vest hid his weapon. "Are y-you…"

Creed dropped my underwear into the drawer and slammed it closed. "Spit it out. Am I what?"

"Are you going to hurt my father? Are you going to kill him?"

He leaned against my vanity, folding his thick arms across his chest. A small eternity later, he lifted a shoulder with a half-hearted shrug, like it was no big deal. "Not if he cooperates."

"And me? Are you going to hurt me?"

I folded my own arms, hiding my hardened nipples from view. Creed flicked his gaze to my bare stomach, causing fire to burn at the back of my neck. "Why would I do that?"

"Because that's what you people do. You cause pain and destruction—"

"More so than your selfish, corrupt father?"

"He's not cor—"

"He's worse than I am," he snapped, pushing off the vanity. I gulped as he sauntered closer, unfolding his large arms. "I slaughter my enemies in the street, witnesses or not. People know what to expect from me. Your father commits his crimes behind the veil of politics and wears a mask to hide his deceit. He's a monster, a wolf in sheep's

6

clothing, but you know that already, don't you?" At my silence, golden rivers of smug, satisfied honey flared in Creed's irises. "What we do to your father is our business. As for you...you're safe for now, little girl."

I bristled, cutting my eyes at him. "Little girl? I'm a woman."

I was. I had credit cards, my own car, and my cup size was well into the Cs. I had no curfew, no sitters, no one to report to so long as I kept a low profile and avoided the press—which wasn't hard in a town like Exeter. I was a woman—albeit a young one—and I had wants and needs like any other. I wanted Creed to see me in the same light I saw him. He made my muscles tight, my nipples hard, and my panties wet. Did I have a similar effect on him? Had it crossed his mind the things we could do—the things he could make me do—while his friend and my father were preoccupied somewhere else in the house? If he kissed me, I'd kiss him back. If he touched me, I wouldn't tell a soul. James Creed dominated every thought and fantasy I'd had since I first laid eyes on him. A crush. He was my first crush, and my untapped hormones had become fixated on him.

He glanced at my braless breasts, barely held inside my crop top. "So you are."

I shifted awkwardly on my feet, but it did nothing to expel the lava in my veins. A small eternity later, Creed dragged his attentive gaze to my vanity and flicked his chin. "Who's that?"

I followed his line of sight, and my tummy tucked and rolled at the photograph of my boyfriend and me at prom. We'd just won prom king and queen. The photo was taken as he gazed adoringly at me, and I was fake smiling so hard it hurt my cheeks. I liked Pierce, but he wasn't what I wanted.

"My boyfriend." I gulped. "Pierce."

"He looks familiar."

"His father is the sheriff."

Creed kissed his teeth and turned his dark, honey stare on me, unimpressed and a little disgusted. "Exeter's sweetheart dating a pig's son, huh?"

Exeter's sweetheart? I straightened my spine. "Sheriff Donovan is a good man."

He bit out a laugh. "Shows how much you know."

"You have so much to say about my father and the sheriff," I snapped, thrill zapping my bones. "What about me?"

"What about you?"

"What derogatory category do I fall under?"

Creed ignored me and sauntered to my vanity again. Without a word, he opened my panty drawer and retrieved the same pink underwear he held moments ago. Closing it, he toyed with the fabric and pinned me with his gaze. It was darker, less playful than before. Reaching into his leather vest and around his waist, he pulled his handgun from his waistband. Adrenaline peaked in my blood, and my chest rose and fell with deep breaths I tried hard to conceal.

"You said I was safe," I whispered on exhale, taking a minute step back.

Desire bubbled inside me as he stalked forward, and it confused me. Even in danger, my body wanted him, so clearly something was wrong with me, with the way I was wired. He short-circuited my system with a smirk and a flash of his eyes. How?

"And you are." He flicked his gun to the floor at my feet. "On your knees, pretty woman."

"Why?"

"I'm supposed to be holding you under duress. Prez would kick my ass if he knew I was up here small talking."

He pointed the gun at me, and my blood refused to run cold, but I did what he asked. I lowered myself to my knees, and he followed, crouching in front of me. His smell was more potent down here, enticing and unhinging me in the most delightful way.

"Like this?" I asked, licking my lower lip.

"Just like that." Creed's eyes flared. "Now slap yourself in the face."

I frowned, sobering. "You're not serious…"

"I can do it for you, if you prefer."

"That's what gets you off, is it? Beating women?"

"Only when they beg." Smirking, he scratched his brow with the barrel of his handgun. "If Judge comes up here and you're not roughed up, we're both gonna be in shit. He'll do it himself, and trust me, you don't want that."

If he was ordered to rough me up, why hadn't he? Could he get into trouble for not doing what he was told? A part of me wanted him to hurt me, to finally feel his touch. Was that psychotic?

"I'm not slapping myself in the face, Creed."

Pleasure flickered across his features as his name fell from my lips. Lowering his gun, he grabbed my wrists and leaned forward, moving them behind my back. My chin grazed his broad shoulder, and I subtly inhaled. Scents of whiskey, oil, and tobacco tickled my nose. I also detected a gentle hint of rose, remnants of a feminine perfume, and it triggered a vicious swirl of jealousy I had no right feeling in my chest. To get away from it, I turned my head to breathe against his neck. Under the collar of his shirt, I caught a glimpse of goosebumps as they prickled along his skin whenever my exhale blew under the fabric. I clenched and unclenched my fists, doing my best to sit still as he bound my wrists. Before long, the lace of my panties bit into my flesh and held me in place. When he pulled back, he touched my face, admiringly, his expression almost sympathetic. I stared back at him, enchanted by his handsome face. He was older than me by a decade at least, and the thought of having his older, muscular body pressed against mine made me shiver. All the things he could do to me…

All the things he could show me…

"You shouldn't look at me like that," Creed warned through hooded lids.

"Like what?"

"Like you want me to peel you out of your panties and do things I shouldn't."

Heat flooded me. It swirled in my cheeks and soaked me between my legs. I didn't know what to say, what to do, so I lowered my head and looked at the carpet. Outside of masturbation, foreplay, and oral, I had limited experience in sex. Not like Creed.

Maybe that set us worlds apart. I couldn't please him. I wouldn't know how.

"You can slap me now…" I uttered.

He hooked his fingers under my chin, forcing my head up. When our gazes locked, he captured my cheeks in his firm grip and kissed me hard. His lips conquered mine until it wasn't enough and he pushed his tongue into my mouth, claiming me, owning me. My head spun, and I melted into him, kissing him back with everything I had.

He broke the kiss, and I gasped.

"Sorry, sweetheart," he whispered then slapped me hard across the face.

I shouted, and my head was tossed to the side as fire began to burn in the wake of his violence. He righted my head with gentle palms, and my eyes welled with tears as I looked at him through the blur.

"Good girl," Creed murmured, smoothing my hair and swiping my cheeks with his thumbs. I closed my eyes and choked on a single sob, but I wasn't sad. I was relieved. I dragged deep inhales through my nose and out through my mouth until I garnered the composure to look at him. When I did, when our eyes locked, blue to honey-whiskey, I felt like a different woman. Was that stupid? I licked my lower lip and tasted my own blood. No one had ever messed me up before or ruined my perfect image. I was the fucking sweetheart of Exeter, and everyone demanded perfection everywhere I went. Not Creed. He had no problem messing my hair, ruining my clothes, or turning my skin pink. And that drove me crazy.

"Look at you," he said, touching my sore lip, the salt from his skin stinging it. "So wild. If you weren't the offspring of such a cunty human being, I'd take you as my bitch."

I balked. A bitch? I wanted to be his woman—his only woman. I wanted to feel his heated skin under my fingertips and for him to cherish it. "I have no interest in being anyone's bitch."

He scowled. "No? You live in a pit full of vipers. Every relationship you've ever had has been superficial and short lived. You wouldn't appreciate the honor of being my bitch."

Creed grabbed his gun, lifted himself to his feet, and turned away. He said *bitch* like it meant something, like it was something to be proud of, and I didn't understand. I sniffled as he stalked to my vanity, took the photo of Pierce and me, and smashed the glass on the surface. Without a glance in my direction, he took it from the frame, ripped it in half, and slipped one half in his pocket. The other he tore into little pieces and scattered them on the floor.

"Creed!" his friend boomed from wherever he was, making me jump. "Let's go."

Stuffing his gun back into his waistband, Creed stomped toward the door.

"Wait!" I called, shuffling forward, lifting myself higher on my knees.

I didn't want him to go. I didn't want to be thrust back into my boring life, into my bubble of perfection where I wasn't allowed an opinion or a single hair out of place. I didn't want to go back to fantasizing about the man in leather and denim who rode a motorcycle so loud it hurt my ears. I didn't want to go back to imagining my boyfriend's touch as his. Creed turned around, a breathtaking frown on his face, and I breathed a sigh of relief.

"What?" he demanded, his nostrils flaring impatiently.

"I'm enjoying your company."

He blinked at me, confused, then barked out a laugh, raking his eyes over me. "You are, aren't you?"

Glancing over his shoulder, he stepped closer then lowered himself to meet me eye to eye. I leaned forward, bringing my chest closer to his, my lips too. "Take me with you."

I was crazy for asking. My father would end Creed and his gang if he took me from my home. Still, I wanted to risk it. Anywhere was better than here.

Creed shook his head. "Can't do that."

"Why? Why not?"

"Creed! Let's fucking go," his friend shouted, closer this time.

Creed lifted himself to his feet and turned away. I watched, deflating by the second, as he sauntered toward my door and pulled it all the way open.

"See ya later, Blondie," he called over his shoulder then crossed the threshold, leaving me alone with a busted lip, bound by a pair of my own panties.

TWO

CREED

Twelve months later

My phone buzzed in my pocket, and I pulled it out, knowing exactly who was calling.

"Yeah?" I answered, leaning my ass against my bike.

"Light it up," Judge ordered. "Then come on back to the clubhouse. Plenty of booze and whores waiting for you."

Hanging up, I took one last drag of my cigarette and flicked it. I watched as it sailed through the air, the red ember glowing with finality. *It was finally over.* The cigarette hit the crumpled pile of piece of shit Klan members who encroached on our turf, and it ignited the gasoline we doused them in. In the blink of an eye, the ground caught fire, and their *not-so-secret* warehouse went up in flames.

"Whoo!" Modo cheered, clapping from his bike. "Fuck you!"

I smirked over my shoulder at him. He sat atop his all-black Triumph Rocket III, draped forward, resting his thick forearms on the handlebars.

"You liked that, did you?" I asked, pushing off my bike.

He grinned. "You know I love fried Klansmen for dinner."

"Just not enough to cook them yourself."

He balked. This was *his* fucking job. I shouldn't be out here. I should be at the clubhouse, relaxing, after chasing four grimy Twisted Sons out of our town last night. Modo was supposed to purge the remaining Nazis and burn the warehouse to the ground. I should be drunk off my ass and balls deep in blondes who resembled the mayor's daughter, but *Modo* couldn't get off his damn bike. Because his dick hurt.

"Hey," he protested. "It's not my fault I pulled my groin—"

"Shouldn't jerk off so much." I swiped at my forehead as sweat built from the heat of the fire.

"Fuck you, Creed. You know I'm not afraid to do dirty work."

He was right. In fact, he loved to do dirty work. Francis, the crazy British bastard, got the nickname "Modo" for feeding his parents to an illegally acquired Komodo Dragon. I didn't know the details, he never told them, but I knew they hurt him, so he hurt them back.

"Just ask his boyfriend," Cyrus quipped, tossing something into the flames.

The boys and I looked at Ayr, Modo's best friend, eyebrows raised.

"Oh, piss off." Ayr scowled, kicking gravel toward our bikes. "I hate you all."

We roared with laughter. Ayr and Modo were far from gay, but we tormented them every chance we got. A siren squealed, and red and blue lights flashed from the dirt road ten feet out. I turned and watched as the sheriff drove by with his deputy in the passenger seat. They glared at us, and we stared back, daring them to get out of their car and fucking try us. We were untouchable. We paid, blackmailed, and threatened Mayor Laurent enough to know we were safe doing our business, as long as we didn't mess with the locals. For the most part, Exeter locals avoided us like the plague, except wild open public nights at the clubhouse—like tonight. Local women came out of the woodwork when our parties were open to them.

As always, the cops continued on their way, knowing better than to get involved in our business. I wished they would, so I could take out all my frustration on the sheriff, who also happened to be the father of a spoiled, handsy, preppy little cunt named *Pierce*. Izzy still dated him. She still lived her life like she didn't ask me to take her away, to make her mine.

Like I promised Judge, I kept my distance, but I saw Blondie in town with Pierce sometimes. In private, late at night, when I was hanging around places I shouldn't, I saw him kiss her with his sloppy, rough lips. I watched him peel her too quickly out of her clothes, not stopping to savor how perfect her body was or how soft she felt in places she kept hidden under flowy fabrics. She was

16

thicker around the thighs and ass, and her breasts were more than I could hold in my hand. *It wasn't fucking fair.* I wanted her the moment I saw her, alone in her room in her underwear. I planned on getting her too, until Judge made her off limits to me. Off-fucking-limits. I'd never been good at following rules, but whatever Judge said went. He was president of our chapter—sometimes a damn ruthless one—and I owed him my life. If he marked a bitch off limits, then that was where she stayed until he said otherwise. So, out of honor and respect, I stayed away and let the pig's son continue to put his disgusting, unappreciative, unworthy hands on her.

"You and Judge still got the mayor under your thumb?" Armi, our Sergeant-at-Arms, asked, sauntering to stand beside me.

I nodded, my stare glued to the taillights. "There's a new election coming up, though, and we need to make sure Laurent wins again."

"If he doesn't?"

A small part of me flared with hope and excitement. If Jonathan Laurent didn't win the next election, Blondie was fair game and all mine.

"If he doesn't, we've got a lot of shit to move before the law comes crashing down on us." I turned toward my bike and threw my leg over it. "It'd only be temporary. Judge would get the next mayor under control eventually."

I started my bike and headed toward the dirt road, eager to leave this complicated Nazi bullshit behind me and get the hell home.

* * *

Laughter erupted from my table. Bottles of beer clashed together, and chairs screeched against the tiled floor. The usually spacious clubhouse was packed to the rafters. There were no familiar faces, just bodies…lots and lots of bodies, crammed in like sardines. It stank in here, like beer, sweat, and fucked pussy.

"Fire's out," Judge announced, and I lifted my head as he slid a fresh, cold beer across the table. It slid effortlessly, clashing lightly with the glass I already had. "The warehouse is a shell, the guts completely burned out of it."

I scooped up my beer and downed the last mouthful, pushing the glass to the side. "Good."

Judge sat across from me and leaned his elbows on the table, his leather cut hanging open.

"That one's giving you the eyes, VP," Casino, our treasurer, said, kicking my boot. "Go say hello. You deserve it after cooking those Nazi cunts."

I turned my head, following his golden stare to a brunette by the bar. I flicked my gaze down the length of her long, slender body, appreciating the way her jeans clung to her legs and her crop top hugged her big breasts.

I grabbed my new beer and drew it to my mouth. "Nah."

"Creed has a type," Judge said, sitting back in his seat, and I cut my eyes at him.

Modo scoffed. "Who has a type? What the hell does that even mean? I'll take any bitch as long as she's got a working pussy."

18

"Yeah, Modo, we know." Casino laughed, his green eyes flashing. "The challenge for you is getting her to want you back."

We laughed as Modo huffed. He told us all to go fuck ourselves and that he could get any bitch in the clubhouse he wanted—if it wasn't for his groin pain, of course.

"What's Creed's type anyway?" Modo asked, looking at Judge, who smirked back at him.

"Young, blonde, and busty," Ayr chimed in, grinning as he lifted his whiskey to his mouth.

I watched, my attention flicking between them as they exposed my attraction to Izzy for Modo to pick apart. They all knew my type, and Modo would too if he bothered to pull his head out of his ass.

"Blue eyes," Casino said.

"And *off* limits," Judge added, pinning me with his stare.

He had to remind me often, especially when I got into one of my moods—like now—when Blondie was all I could think about. Lifting himself out of his seat, he sauntered across the room to the poles where topless thong-clad clubsluts danced, drank, and waited for a member to choose them.

"Christ, VP. You still hooked on Laurent's daughter?" Modo snorted, and I turned my head to look at him. "She's sexy, but—"

"But what?" I bit out, clenching my beer.

He stroked his ridiculously long copper beard. "I don't think she's all there—in the head, I mean."

Ayr and Casino sucked air between their teeth as I thinned my eyes. Was he serious? Of all the people to comment on someone's mental capacity, it was the dumbest asshole I knew?

"You've never fucking met her," I pointed out, and he exposed his palms, as if I were a wild animal he needed to pacify.

"I know, but I've seen her, and she seems…"

"Shut up, Modo," Ayr hissed, pinching the bridge of his nose.

"Dumb. She seems dumb, you know?" I lifted my eyebrows as he turned to his best friend. "What do you think, Ayr?"

"I think you should shut your stupid mouth before VP murders you."

Modo looked at me, completely oblivious to the issue. "But do you understand what I'm saying?"

Casino cursed, shifting in his seat. "We understand what you're saying. You haven't been vague."

"At all," Ayr added.

"I've seen bricks that look smarter than that bitch—"

Growling, I shoved the table at him, breaking cups and spilling everyone's drinks. Casino and Ayr shot back in their seats, swearing and shouting as good beer was wasted and their clothes were wet.

"You don't know shit," I ground out, adding pressure.

Modo gripped the edge of the table, his teeth bared as he sucked air between them. He tried to push back, but I held it steady. He was tough as nails, damn psychotic when he was mad, but I was stronger. I was vice president for a goddamn reason.

"Ah, fuck. My ribs."

A piercing whistle cut through my ears, and I

grimaced, whipping around to face the sound. Judge approached us, his expression pinched in a frown. "You know the rules. You wanna fight, take it outside, or I'll have Armi kick the shit out of the both of you."

"Well." Modo exhaled, pushing the table away from him until it bumped my thigh. "I would, but I pulled a—"

I groaned. "If I hear you say that one more time—"

"What? It's true."

I'd die for my brothers, any one of them, but Modo was the most annoying motherfucker this side of the U.S. He had no filter, no standards, and no self-control, *but* he was a maniac who wielded a killer axe, and we needed that.

Hanging onto Judge's cut, a tiny blonde woman caught my attention and stared up at me. She wasn't a natural blonde, and she didn't have big tits, but she was pretty—for a patchwhore. Funnily enough, I was never a man who had a type—any willing hole was a goal—until I met Isabelle. That night, she was ready to throw it all away for me. *I should've taken her, should've made her mine*, but a beautiful young thing like her had no business being with a bad man like me. I was no good, rotten to the core. I killed my first man at thirteen—my uncle. Got sick of him beating my aunt, so I sank a kitchen knife into the back of his neck. Afterward, my aunt did everything in her power to have me locked up for murder, even denied the brutal beatings my uncle gave her. I didn't understand why she protected him and threw me under the bus, still

21

didn't, but it wasn't all bad. I ended up in a maximum-security detention center, where I met Judge. He killed someone, too, but he never told me who it was.

"I picked her myself," Judge said, pulling me from my thoughts as he pushed the woman toward me.

His voice was confident, like he knew I wouldn't turn him down. Valid, since I hadn't turned his offerings down in the past. He knew I liked them blonde, no plastic, no piercings, no ink. I needed them looking as close to Blondie as possible—for selfish reasons *and* for business reasons. After I finished with them, I took photos and texted them to Laurent from a burner phone to keep him on his toes.

The woman switched to me without protest and touched my tattooed arms, rubbing her naked body against me. It should be enough to get me going, but I wasn't in the right headspace. I got no sleep last night and spent the first half of tonight beating Nazis to death. All I wanted to do was drink and sleep.

I pressed my hand to the small of the woman's back and pushed her toward Judge.

"Not in the mood," I said, and she pouted.

"Jesus, Creed," Modo shouted. "That's not a type. It's a fucking fetish."

This asshole. I pushed past them and headed toward the front door in need of fresh air before I got another drink. The gyrating crowd parted for me, not wanting to get caught in my way or crushed under my heavy boots.

"Where are you going?" Judge called after me.

"For a piss," I shouted over my shoulder. "Why, you wanna watch?"

"Fuck off, Creed."

My lips twitched as I exited the clubhouse and stepped into the cool, fresh night air.

THREE

IZZY

"Drink this," Chelsea says, tossing a can of citrus-twist vodka at me. "Then get dressed. You're coming with me."

I catch it awkwardly in my hands and grimace. "Dad will kill me."

I'm banned from going to the west side of Exeter where the enigmatic men in leather run wild. If I went to the Devil's Cartel clubhouse, my father wouldn't *just* kill me. He'd use tweezers to pick me apart in tiny increments until my death, then he'd find a way to resurrect me and do it all again. Not a meal went by he didn't curse their existence and threaten to bury them all. Damon Judge had my father under his thumb, and Dad loathed it, but it was James Creed who really made Dad boil. Maybe he knew about the kiss or that I asked Creed to take me with him. Maybe he's heard me moan Creed's name in my sleep whenever he plagued my dreams.

"You're an adult," Chelsea states, pulling the

skirt of her cherry red dress down her thighs. The shimmery fabric clings to her muscles like a second skin, accentuating the curve of her backside. "Who cares what your dad thinks?"

I crack the seal on the can and take a sip. The lemony flavor tickles my tongue and stimulates my glands as the liquid bubbles and burns at my mouth. "If I'm seen there having fun, how would that look? It'd ruin my father's whole campaign—"

"Still not your problem." She exhales, pulling her long, chocolate hair over one slender shoulder, and sits on the bed beside me, taking my hands in hers, spilling a few drops of my drink. They soak into my black jeans. "I'm leaving town, Iz. This is the last night we're going to spend together for a long, *long* time. I've always respected your decision not to come to the clubhouse in the past, but *girl*, come on. Just this once."

I look at her furrowed brow and pouty lips then stare into her round, pleading brown eyes. My thoughts begin to swirl, and my heart picks up in its beat at the thought of being close to Creed again, at the thought of being in his territory instead of the safety of my room.

I catch my lower lip between my teeth then release it, pulling my hands free.

"Fine," I say, blowing air from my lips. I bring the can to my mouth and swallow two large mouthfuls. "I'll come, but I'm using you as a scapegoat if he finds out."

Chelsea beams, pulling her closed fists under her jaw and squealing with delight. "We're going to have so much fun!"

She lifts off her king-sized bed and dances along the floor to her walk-in closet. I watch helplessly, drinking my drink as she tosses dress after dress onto the floor. I try to focus on what she's saying— what colors would match my skin tone, what hairstyle would better frame my face—but all I can think about is Creed. Exhilaration runs hot in my veins and lifts fine hair off my skin. My crush on him has only intensified since the last time I saw him—a lifetime ago now—and Pierce and I are on a break. At my discretion, I could have Creed tonight. I finish off my can and reach for another as a wicked plan formulates through the nervousness in my belly.

I *will* have Creed tonight.

* * *

"Awooooo!" A ferocious howl rips through the air, piercing my eardrums.

I scream, grabbing onto Chelsea's arm as a group of four rush by us, laughing, eager to get to the overflowing clubhouse.

"Scared me," I say on exhale, earning a snicker from my best friend.

I release Chelsea's arm and press my palm to my chest to feel my heart as it slams into my ribcage. I'm so far out of my comfort zone it's terrifying. Only once has my heart beat this fast.

"Won't be the last time. These parties get pretty wild." She peers sideways at me, grinning. "Who knows? Maybe you'll end up screaming in someone's ear tonight, too."

Her implication doesn't pass me by. I pull a face, but my mind is already traveling down that road. I know I shouldn't be contemplating tracking down Creed and getting him alone, since Pierce and I haven't officially broken up, but...it's Creed. It's always been Creed for me.

Chelsea escorts me down the gentle grassy slope and onto a wide path of flat gravel that leads to the monstrous clubhouse. I rake my gaze over the huge building that towers over us. It's a converted warehouse that could fit well over half the town's population. Chelsea gives me a quick rundown, and according to her, most of the men live here. There are sections of the clubhouse that are off limits, and she rattles them off, but I'm not paying attention. I'm consumed by the giant bonfire in the middle of the field one hundred yards out and the men and women who walk back and forth, dressed in leather, denim, and dark fabrics.

"Don't ever go in there. No one is allowed in their rooms unless they choose you."

I nod, though I have no idea who or what she's talking about. "Okay."

"Also, there's a few you need to avoid, like Modo and—"

I zone her out as a tall man with salt and pepper hair winks at me, lifting his drink as he saunters by. *So friendly.* I follow him with my gaze and suck air between my teeth at the sight of the gigantic devil-skull on his back and the words that circle it. *Devil's Cartel. California.* Thrill zips down my spine. I can't believe I'm here. At *their* clubhouse. I don't belong here in my baby pink dress. I

27

should've worn the black one like Chelsea suggested, but I thought this would remind Creed of our exchange a year ago.

"If they get handsy," Chelsea continues, "tell them you're a member of the public, not a—"

"Mhm," I hum, flicking my lagging gaze over everything in sight, inhaling the gritty, delightful smells as I go.

Rock music plays, it blasts from speakers mounted on the clubhouse, and the harsh beats demolish the classical tastes my father instilled in me from birth. Mozart who? Beethoven who? Give me the man screaming so hard his vocal cords sound like they're tearing apart. Give me electric guitars that squeal in pain and drums that pound louder than thunder.

I'm shouldered by an angry man I don't see, and somewhere in the distance, motorcycles roar to life, the sounds of their engines burying under my skin. Overwhelming tears blur my vision, and I smile as we approach the entrance where two men shout. The tallest man, the one with his leather sleeves cut off, showcasing his umber skin and thick biceps, towers over a shorter man in a faded tee. I don't know what they're saying or what a Triumph is, but they don't agree, and they're not afraid to make noise.

"And that's all you need to know," Chelsea shouts in my ear. "Any questions?"

Questions? "Uh—"

The front doors are thrown open, and a man is hurtled out. Chelsea and I stumble backward as he hits the ground and rolls to a stop in front of our feet, groaning and clutching his ribs.

"I won't tell you again, fucker!" the biker at the top of the four steps shouts, pointing a long, thick finger at the man on the ground. "You're not welcome here."

Excitement crackles in the air and crepitates over my scalp as I gawk at the blond, long-haired biker. The men who live out here, scurrying around in the dark while the rest of us sleep, are something else, and I'm attracted to it, to the lifestyle, to the thought of being an outlaw and having no one to answer to.

"You!" the biker booms, pointing his long, thick finger at Chelsea. "Get your sexy ass up here."

She starts forward, stepping over the man in front of us, who moans and rolls flat on his back. I follow, stepping over his legs, and snag her forearm out of panic.

"Don't leave me alone."

"You'll be fine if you follow what I told you."

I widen my eyes. *What did she tell me?*

"I'll come find you in a little while and we can spend the rest of the night together."

She plants a swift kiss on my cheek then rushes up the steps to the tall, handsome biker. Her long, chocolate locks reach the middle of her back and bounce with every step, the skirt of her red dress tightly hugging her curves. The biker forcefully grabs and hoists her like she weighs nothing. Chelsea squeals in delight as he throws her over his shoulder and lifts her dress to palm her ass, revealing her black thong. Heat floods my cheeks, and I look away.

Maybe I am out of my depth here...

"You should know," the man on the ground groans, peeking up my dress. Disgusted, I step away, and he grins at me, still clenching his ribs. "*A little while* can be hours in patchrider time."

"Patchrider?"

"Don't play coy, girl. Clubwhore. Patchwhore. Clubslut—"

I walk away, heading toward the entrance of the clubhouse where Chelsea and the biker entered. Chelsea isn't a *clubwhore*. She doesn't need this club. She's rich, ridiculously so, and beautiful, and well on her way to running her own haute couture fashion empire. I imagine her obsession with this place is only because it infuriates her father, who happens to be a famous Los Angeles attorney. She's twisted like that—all my friends are. I guess I am, too. My therapist knows of my obsession with Creed, with leather, lace, loud engines, and burning rubber. He thinks it grew from my father's overprotectiveness and fear of these gritty men. He thinks it's a fantasy I'll grow out of or forget once I try it, but I'm not so sure. It's probably stupid, a ridiculous notion that's stemmed from a teenage infatuation, but there's an invisible thread that ties me to Creed. I want him—*bad*. I want him so bad I'd give up every luxury I have just to kiss him again, to taste the darkness on his tongue.

I open one of the huge clubhouse doors and step inside, coming face to face with another biker. I gasp, my eyebrows lifting to my hairline, and I flick my attention down her slim waist and wide hips. I look at her big leather boots, skinny denim jeans, and black V-neck tee, then I survey her leather vest.

It looks real. It has the scary, circular skull patch on the breast and everything. *She's a part of the gang?* Under the warm lights above, her umber skin glows with ochre highlights, and her hair is pulled back tight, her natural curls a soft, elegant ball on the top of her head. I swallow hard. I've never seen a complexion so flawless, without a single bump, a single blemish. Like all the club members, she's intimidating, even more so since she's a woman in a man's club. *How'd she get here? What'd she do to get in?* I read online that women can't be patched into outlaw clubs like this. I also noticed most clubs only had white members—other Devil's Cartel chapters included. Maybe Damon Judge isn't as big an asshole as people make him out to be.

She tilts her head, her face a perfect picture of feigned sympathy.

"Oh, honey, *pink*?" She reaches out with her slender fingers and touches my dress then my long, blonde hair. "They're going to eat you alive."

I frown. "They?"

"They," she repeats, laughing as she slaps my shoulder and leaves the building.

I turn my attention to the room and feel blood drain from my face. Clashing of glasses, roaring of laughter, stomping of boots, and moaning of men and women alike flood my ears. It's one thing to hear stories, but it's another thing entirely to witness the way they live. It's barbaric. Twisted.

Exhilarating.

I'm pulled from my train of thought by a smack on my ass. I yelp, shooting forward, smoothing my hands over my backside, and I snap my head to look over my shoulder.

"You're blocking the door, baby," an old man in a black denim jacket shouts in my ear.

He presses his hand to my lower back and eases me to the side before stalking into the crowd, disappearing completely. *What the hell?* I take a deep breath, trying to remember Chelsea's rules. *Who am I supposed to avoid? What am I supposed to say? And where do I find Creed?*

I stick to the edge of the clubhouse, going unnoticed as I slip by grinding men and women who have no shame fucking where everyone can see. By some miracle, I make it across the giant space unhindered and stop at a large oak bar. Sighing in relief, I place one foot on the rest of the stool next to me and lean on my elbows. *I need a drink.* The vodka twists I drank at Chelsea's are quickly wearing off, and I'm losing my nerve.

"What do you want?" a young man demands, rushing toward me from behind the bar, impatience and irritation wafting off him in waves.

He's younger than most here, younger than me even, and he's clearly a part of the club, but he wears a brown vest instead of black.

"Oh." I flick my hand at him. "I don't want to bother you. It's fine."

"Can't have you standing here taking up space," he says, his voice tinged with an accent that reminds me of my time in Australia. "Order a drink or piss off."

Rude. "Okay...I'll have a cosmopolitan, please."

Those close enough to hear my order roar with laughter. I frown at them as they look me up and down. I can tell immediately they don't take me seriously, that they think I'm some dumb wannabe who doesn't belong. They're right, but still. Where's the discretion?

"A cosmopolitan?" the bartender says, throwing a towel over his shoulder. "Are you lost, Barbie? This isn't the fucking Ten Pound Bar."

I'm impressed he knows the Ten Pound Bar. It's my favorite place to go whenever I'm in Beverly Hills.

"Why ask me what I want if I can't have it?"

"You can have Jack, Jim, Johnny, Jose, or beer—and not that low-carb shit, either."

"Give me Jack," I say with absolute confidence, though I have no idea what it'll taste like.

I'm a cocktail girl. I drink things that have fancy names, come in different colors, and are garnished with fresh fruit. In less than two minutes, he slides a rocks glass of liquid that reminds me of Creed's irises in front of me. Curious, I lift the glass and peer through the liquid. I don't need to touch my nose to the rim to smell it. It's potent, even from a few inches away.

"Where do I pay for this?" I ask, wondering why he hasn't asked for my card.

"Booze is on the house for patchriders tonight—provided you're actually out there fucking."

"Patchriders..."

He thinks I'm a clubwhore. I smooth my features out, deadpanning. This is getting old, *fast*.

Exhaling, I sit the glass on the bar and pull my credit card from a subtle pocket on the inside of my soft, fabric bodice.

"I said drinks are free for patch—"

"I'm not one of *those*," I snap, dropping my card to the bar's surface.

The bartender, *prospect* it says on his breast, arches an eyebrow as I scoop up my glass.

"Charge me for three," I tell him, swallowing my current drink in one large mouthful, gritting my teeth as it burns my throat. "And bring them to me."

He does what he's told, and when he comes back, he returns my card and leans on the bar.

"You look familiar." He holds out his hand. "I'm Kace."

I place my hand in his, and he grips it tight, a firm shake.

"Isabelle Laurent."

Flinching, he drops my hand like a hot poker then zips forward to snatch my drinks away. I quickly pull them back, leaning away from the bar.

"What's your problem?" I demand, my head already spinning from my first glass of Jack.

"I shouldn't have given you those." Kace shakes his head then pushes his tattooed fingers over his shaved skull. "You can't have 'em."

"Why not?"

"Because your Isabelle-*fucking*-Laurent and I'm not allowed to—"

"Says who?"

"Judge. Creed."

My heart rate picks up at the mention of his name. I haven't seen him since that night. I was beginning to wonder if I'd imagined our exchange, that Creed was a cruel illusion conjured from a bored and lonely heart. "Where can I find him?"

"Judge?"

"Creed."

Kace cuts his eyes at me. "You should go home."

"If you tell me where I can find him, I'll give your drinks back."

He tilts his head. Kace can't be much older than twenty. His face is boyish, his eyes kind and inexperienced, much like the boys I went to school with.

"And if I don't tell you?"

Lifting one rocks glass to my lips, I tip the two fingers of Jack into my mouth and swallow, making a rough, gross noise in my throat. "I'll drink them all, strip naked, and run around screaming your name."

"You wouldn't."

I arch an eyebrow, daring him to try me. He doesn't budge. Hell, he barely looks phased by my threat. Flicking my tongue along the front of my teeth, I sigh and reach for the strap of my dress. I push it halfway down my bicep before Kace slams his palm against the oak surface.

"All right." He curses. "Down the hall, last door on the right. Creed should be in his room."

I smile. "Thank you."

I turn in the direction of the hall on the other side of the room. Kace clears his throat, and I glance over my shoulder. He holds out his hand, and I roll my eyes. I begin to hand the glass over when a strange apprehension seizes my chest. If I'm going to Creed's room, in a place where naked whores drip from every fixture, waiting to fuck anyone with a patch, I'll need this drink. He could have someone with him…

I slam back the alcohol and toss the empty rocks glass into Kace's waiting hand. He shouts my name, calls me a lying bitch, but I'm already pushing my way through the drunken, sweaty crowd.

In the empty hall that leads to the Devil's Cartel sleeping quarters, an open door at the far end draws my attention. I catch a glimpse of a skull and flames insignia on a broad back before the man disappears behind a closing door. My heart races, my chest rising and falling with shallow breaths. Everything goes quiet, the sounds of the clubhouse fading to nothing, as the thundering of my pulse becomes the dominate sound. *Did Kace say Creed's room is on the left- or the right-hand side?* I rub the back of my neck. *I really need to start listening to people better.* I don't imagine these men will be lenient with me if I end up in the wrong place. I glance over my shoulder. What if I see something I shouldn't? Would they kill me? I gulp and shake the thoughts from my head. I'm only going into a bedroom. What's the worst that can happen, really? Going against my better judgment, I stroll down the hall to the last door on the left, and with liquid courage in my veins, I open it and slip inside.

FOUR

IZZY

I hold my breath as I press my back against the cold, lacquered plywood. It's dark, so dark I can't see, and my eyes fail to adjust. Exhaling, I step forward, only to be slammed back against the door. My skull connects first, sending pain into my eye sockets, then the rest of me hits. I shout and catch a strong, impossibly thick forearm to the throat. My windpipe compresses, and I thrash to no avail as pressure builds in my face, like an over-inflated balloon. I feel the cold tip of a blade against my throat then, threatening to fillet me like a fish. I still as tears pool in my eyes. *I shouldn't have snuck in. I shouldn't've caught him off guard.* A pathetic whimper squeezes from my lips, and he tenses then pulls the blade away and removes his forearm. I gasp for air, grasping at my throat as he gropes my breasts, making sure I'm a woman.

"Oh my God," I whisper, letting out a nervous laugh. "I thought you were going to kill—"

I hear the blade clash with something across the room, and I squeak as I'm ripped from the floor and lifted into strong arms.

"Cr—"

He crushes his mouth to mine, pushing his tongue inside and claiming me like a starving man. I kiss him back, wrapping my arms around his neck and my legs around his waist. He's thicker than I remember, and taller, but he smells the same—like leather, rubber, and asphalt. On his tongue, I taste Jack, and I've never loved the flavor more. Creed holds me by my bare thighs, the tips of his fingers grazing between my legs, caressing the flimsy fabric that separates our flesh.

Groaning, he breaks the kiss, and my stomach sinks as I'm thrown from his arms. I free fall for a moment before I'm caught by a soft mattress. *Jesus. How can he see anything?*

"You don't want to talk first?" I ask on exhale.

Large, rough hands engulf my ankles and yank me down the bed, then I'm flipped onto my stomach. I gulp air as my head spins, more alcohol seeping into my blood every second. I rest my cheek against the blanket as he palms my ass and pulls my panties to the side. Heat rushes between my legs, my arousal pooling and unbearable. Pierce never made me feel like this—overheated, overwhelmed, and naughty. *So naughty.*

Creed presses a finger to my clit then drags it toward my entrance. I close my eyes, my breath hitching, as the very tip of his finger breaches me. Groaning, I arch my back, sticking my ass out, wanting more, wanting him to give me more.

"You like that, do you?" He leans over to speak in my ear. My eyes shoot open, and the arousal I feel turns from sparkles to spiders on my skin. "You know you're not allowed in my room. Now I'm gonna punish you."

He doesn't sound anything like Creed. "Wait!"

I squeeze my arms under my body and try to lift myself, but the man above me drops more of his weight.

"Not in the mood to play out your rape fantasy tonight, Liv."

The biker, whoever it is, takes his finger from my entrance and grinds his pelvis into my ass, pushing his hard bulge between my ass cheeks.

"Wait," I plead again, exhausting myself trying to push against him. "I'm not—"

He covers my mouth, and the subsequent sound of his zipper is deafening. I growl so hard my vocal cords burn in my throat, then I wrench my head to the side, causing his hand to slip.

"Get the hell off me!" I shout then bite his hand, sinking my teeth deep into his flesh.

"Ah!" he hollers, ripping his hand free and lifting himself off me. "What the fuck is your problem, you crazy bitch?"

In the darkness, I lift myself on shaky arms and scramble to adjust my clothes. Heavy boots, boots that sound like Creed's, hit the ground as whoever it is storms away. I manage to rake my fingers through my hair before I'm blinded by the warm bedroom light. Hissing, I shield my eyes with my hand against my brow bone and find myself squinting into furious dark, ocean blue irises. My stomach turns. I drag my stare down his impossibly tall, impossibly wide frame and back up again, my attention resting on the patch sewn into the front of his leather vest. *President.* I grimace. *Damon Judge.*

"What the fuck are *you* doing here?" he booms, startling me as he zips his dark, worn jeans.

"I-I was looking for someone else. I thought you were…" I swallow hard. "Someone else."

Judge cuts his eyes at me, sneering. "Creed?"

I shake my head, but heat rushes to my cheeks, betraying me. I can't hide what I feel for James Creed. Not only is it written all over my face, but Judge felt it in the warmth emanating from between my thighs; he felt it in the wetness he happily collected from my body. If it were Creed, we'd already be a tangled mess of sexual energy. I'd have begged him to take me, pleaded with him to fuck me harder than I've ever been fucked.

"Forget that, *Blondie.*" Judge pushes his fingers through his cropped, jet black hair. "It's not gonna happen between you and Creed. *Ever.*"

I frown. "Why?"

"Because I said so." He approaches me, towers over me, and flicks his hand toward my dress, scowling. "You didn't even try to blend in. Why the fuck are you wearing pink?"

"No one told me there was a dress code…"

"Does your father know you're here?" I shake my head, and he grabs my face, squeezing my cheeks so hard my teeth hurt. "This isn't a fucking game. I'll cut your pretty tongue out of your mouth if you lie to me, understand?"

I nod.

"Does your father know you're here?" he asks again, emphasizing each word.

"No."

He relaxes his shoulders a little, staring into my eyes. "You been drinking?"

I nod again. "Yes."

"Drugs?"

I shake my head, and he releases his grip on my face with an irritated shove. Blowing air between my lips, I massage my jaw. He turns away, pulling a cell phone from his back pocket. He taps at the screen with his thumbs then lifts it to his ear. My heart leaps into my chest at the thought of him calling Creed. Will he hate me? Even though it was an accident? Maybe, after all this time, he won't care. I don't know what'll hurt me more.

"Armi," Judge barks into the phone. "My room. *Now.*"

Judge crosses the uncluttered and surprisingly spacious room to a small bar on the other side. I stand awkwardly and glance around his private space. It's clean and coordinated with its expensive fittings and monochrome color scheme. It reminds me of a prison cell, an elegant and comfortable one, but a cell all the same.

I'm pulled from my thoughts by a gentle waft of cigarette flowing from Judge's direction. He simmers in silence, pacing back and forth, burning through his cigarette like no one's business. I remain silent, not wanting to set him off. He's intimidating, powerful, and he's built like a bull. He'd crush me in a heartbeat.

There's a knock at the door, and Judge grumbles

for Armi to come in. I nervously shift my weight and wrap my arm around my waist to hold my elbow as the handle is pulled down and the door opens. The biker, a tall, dirty-blond man with an athletic build, steps inside and closes the door behind him. His long hair is disheveled, hanging messily around his face, blending in with his short beard.

"Prez?" he says, dragging his attention from the wide expanse of Judge's back to me. His dark eyes widen, and I shrink under his unwelcoming gape. "Is that—"

"How the fuck did she get in?" Judge demands, whipping around to face us.

"I didn't see her."

"You didn't see her? She's wearing pink!"

Armi extends his arm and points at the door. "There's a thousand fucking people out there."

"I don't give a shit." Judge flicks his head in my direction. "Get her home in one piece. Use your truck, not your bike. I don't want Jonathan to know she was here with us. Dealing with that asshole is the last thing I need right now."

I frown. "Is that why I'm not welcome here? Because of my father?"

"All right," Armi says on exhale, ignoring me. "Can she wait by the garage for fifteen minutes? I gotta sort Kace out. He got into it with some preppy assholes, and Iris—"

"Hurry up." Judge flicks his head, and Armi leaves. Then he turns his attention to me. "Don't utter a word about this," he warns. "Not to your whore friend, not to your father, not to Creed."

42

I cut my eyes at him and straighten my shoulders. A bratty retort dances on my tongue, and I plan on spitting it at him until he steps forward, and fear seizes me. I step back and nod, quickly.

"I won't say anything," I promise. *I just want to get out of here.* "I won't tell anyone."

He stares me down, his blue eyes flicking between mine, searching for the truth in my words. Whether or not he finds it, I don't know. Sneering, he waves me off.

"Get out of my sight, *girl*, and don't come back."

Not needing to be told twice, I rush out of the room without a glance over my shoulder.

C R E E D

I leaned against the wall, my leg bent at the knee, tired as shit. In front of me, two topless bitches made out by the poles, encouraged by the men that surround them—patch members and normies alike. Most of the time, we kept the gritty, dirty biker stuff behind closed doors, but I guess it was all out on show tonight. I swallowed the remaining mouthful of my umpteenth beer, the last drop stoking the fire this lesbian show ignited in me. *Maybe I do need to get laid...*

Iris, our female prospect, strolled in front of me, holding a full tray of glasses stacked eight high. Her long, dead-straight black hair swung around her shoulders as she huffed at me, and my lips quirked. At a glance, Iris didn't belong here. She was a tiny Japanese beauty all of nineteen and came as a package deal with Kace, but she proved herself when she outshot Armi at the shooting range. I didn't know her story, but the girl had some serious weapons training. That was all I cared about.

"How much longer is this party gonna go for, VP?" she asked, pouting her full, red lips. "I'm tired."

I placed my cup on top of the tallest stack and smiled down at her. Iris had a fire swirling in her black lagoon irises. She was getting sick of this prospect business, I knew. She wanted more; she wanted the black leather and the patch, and she wanted to get her new motorcycle and go on rides.

But she had to prove her worth first, like everyone else.

"Give the tray to Kace and take the rest of the night off." *Admittedly, I babied her from time to time.* "Stay in your room and lock the door. You don't know who's walking around."

"I have guns in my room."

I shook my head. "Armi took them back to the armory. Prospects aren't permitted loaded weapons in their quarters. You know that." Iris cut her eyes at me, and I lifted an eyebrow, daring her to argue. "You're lucky I talked him out of fining you," I added.

She wouldn't've been able to afford the fine after paying her dues this week. Nodding, Iris sauntered off, and I went back to scouting the talent, looking for a soft-bodied woman to have for the night. Then I spotted *her*. Isabelle Laurent. In my fucking clubhouse, wearing *pink* of all goddamn colors.

Modo saddled up next to her, brushing her hair away from her face. She smiled politely, dragging her sexy fucking gaze up his chest and over his stupid long hair. I was storming across the building before I could register it, a possessive rage bursting in my chest. *I will cut his fingers off then shove them up his ass, one by one.* Smart people jumped out of my way when they saw me approach. The stupider ones I had to shove. When I reached the table, I slammed my hand down on it, making Blondie jump out of her skin and clench her chest. I felt her stare burn into my face the second her beautiful blue orbs landed on me, and it took everything I had to keep my attention on Modo. Hell, it took everything I had not to throw this table over my shoulder, rip her out of her pink dress, and fuck her in her seat so everyone in the room knew who she belonged to.

"This one is *mine*," I told him, my voice dead calm.

Modo lifted his brows, amused. "Thought you weren't in the mood? Besides, don't see your name on it."

It. Don't shoot him, I thought. *You promised Judge you wouldn't shoot him again.* As if he heard my thoughts, Modo rubbed at his shoulder—the same one I shot two years ago.

I exhaled subtly then whirled on my heel and headed for the bar. When I got there, Kace ran up to me, his eyes scanning the crowd. The black bruise quickly swallowing up his left eye didn't pass me by. The idiot was always getting into fights over Iris. I didn't know their history, but I knew they shared a bed every night, cuddling like two love birds.

"Have you seen Iris?"

"Probably getting fucked in a dark corner somewhere," I told him, knowing it'd piss him off. He was possessive of Iris, and I liked to torment him. "Marker," I demanded, tapping the wood. "*Now*."

Swallowing his anger, he reached under the bar and retrieved a black Sharpie. I snatched it out of his palm and made my way back to Modo and Izzy. My stare found hers immediately, and she didn't blink as I approached. I popped the lid off the Sharpie with my thumb, letting it fall to the ground. Then, when my thighs hit the tall table, I leaned over and scrawled my name across her chest, across her breasts. She gasped, her gaze never leaving my face. *JAMES CREED.* Satisfied, I tossed the marker over my shoulder and pinned Modo with a glare.

"Can you read that?"

Modo shrugged, lifting his beer to his mouth. "Barely. Your handwriting is shit."

I smiled. He'd always been a sore loser. From my peripheral, Armi and Casino casually approached.

"Get up, Blondie."

I didn't want any of them looking at her, didn't want any of them talking to her. I wasn't insecure. I knew I had everything she wanted, but I also knew Blondie had a penchant for men like us. So quick her fear turned to desire that night in her room. I remembered it as if it was yesterday. She inhaled me deep into her lungs while I bound her hands behind her back with a pair of her soft, pink lace panties. She could have anyone in the building she wanted, but it'd be over my dead body.

Isabelle did as she was told, lifting herself out of the seat beside Modo, and quickly ambled to stand next to me. She stood close, so close her arm brushed mine. I wished I wasn't wearing a hoodie under my cut. I wanted to feel her.

"Wait. That's Laurent's daughter?" Modo asked, raking his amber eyes up the length of her fit body.

"No," I lied, but Izzy was already nodding.

"Yes, I'm Isabelle," she said, all cute like.

"Jesus, VP." He ate her up with his hungry stare, devouring every inch of her over-exposed, sun-kissed skin. I straightened my shoulders, daring him to say something stupid. "Then who's the blonde with the lip scar and the eyebrow tattoo?"

Eyebrow tattoo? I glanced at Casino, who scowled at Modo. "That's my little sister, asshole."

"Oh." Modo sat back in his seat and grinned at me. "Well, that explains a lot."

"If you think Casino's sister is ugly, there's something wrong with you," Armi chimed in.

"I said dumb, not ugly."

Casino huffed and stuffed his hands inside the pockets of his cut. His was newer than the rest of ours. He'd only been treasurer a few months since our last guy, Geeves, was murdered by the Valkyries in Venton Vale. Geeves' death was yet to be avenged, thanks to Hawk's history with them, but they'd get what's coming eventually.

"Dumb?" Casino bit out. "She's an engineer at NASA, you fucking cabbage."

Modo laughed. "Shit. She must have a killer pussy because there's no way she got there on her intelligence—"

Casino launched at him, diving over the table. Gasping, Izzy grabbed my covered wrist, sending electric currents over my skin, and slipped behind me.

"Should we call the police?" she shouted over sounds of flesh pummeling flesh and eighties rock music as it carried through the clubhouse.

"Nah," I said. "Armi's got it."

Sure enough, when Armi was satisfied Modo got the beating he deserved for talking shit about Casino's sister, Shyloh, he pulled the table out of the way and ripped Casino off him then turned to me. "Prez told me to get her out of here. You mind babysitting for five minutes while I sort this mess out?"

In the depths of Armi's eyes, I saw he was doing me a favor by giving me a few minutes alone with her. *The damage I could do in a few minutes.* I was loyal to Judge, did everything he requested of me, but to be alone with Izzy? And keep my hands to myself? My fingers ached at the thought.

Despite the excitement burrowing through my muscles, I scowled at Armi. I didn't want to babysit *her.* I was fucking vice president, so he shouldn't've asked me in the first place...but I didn't want to leave her with anyone else.

Outside was quieter than inside, the air cooler. We walked side by side toward the gravel drive and the adjacent parking lot, away from everyone else and the raging bonfire yards away.

"You shouldn't be here." I glanced down, and

her lips quirked in the dusky, murky streetlight in front of us. "Lots of bad men out tonight."

"Like you?" she teased, keeping her gaze forward, and hair lifted from my skin.

"Especially me."

What was it about her that made every cell in my being come alive? I'd been around women my whole life—been with more women than I cared to count. I didn't recall wanting anyone the way I wanted Isabelle. Armi thought it was because Judge made her off limits, said I was a spoiled, arrogant asshole who got off on being told no. Maybe he was right, or maybe I felt renewed by Isabelle's youth. Her innocence, and the excitement she stirred in me, reminded me of the boy I was before I was fucked over by my family and the system.

"I'm not scared of you," she said.

"No?" I smirked, slowing to a stop, and leaned against the clubhouse wall. If she had any idea what I'd done in my life—what I continued to do—she'd stop romanticizing me and start fearing me instead. "You should be."

"Why? Are you still breaking into houses and slapping women in their bedrooms?"

I laughed at her quip, at the warmth spreading through my face, and shrugged. "Old habits die hard."

Izzy turned in my direction and stepped closer, hugging herself. "Is that right?"

She looked perfect with her long, blonde hair that wildly framed her beautiful face. Her long lashes, high cheekbones, and full lips drove home the fact she'd grown up a lot in the last year. Her appearance was more mature, more refined, like she knew what she wanted and wasn't afraid to take it. And her big tits, sitting braless in the pathetic fabric of her pink dress, her hard nipples threatening to cut through? *Fuck.* If Armi didn't get here soon, I was gonna do something bad.

"I searched all over for you," she admitted, flicking her stare over my face.

"But you couldn't find me, so you settled for Modo instead."

The words left my mouth without prior thought as jealousy flared inside me. Izzy bit back a smile, thrilled by the harsh tone of my voice. I'd given it all away with my sentence, in my tenor, how much I cared, how sick it made me to see her with someone else. Clearing my throat, I reached into my pocket and pulled out my cell, checking the time. We'd already been alone six minutes.

"He's interesting," she thought aloud, turning her head toward the long, silent road across the drive. "Charming, almost."

I dragged my stare down the slope of her neck to her chest and imagined kissing her there, between her full breasts where my name stained her skin. *Torture.* I stuffed my cell into the pocket of my jeans and shrugged out of my cut then pulled my hoodie over my head.

"Here," I said, handing it to her. "It's cold."

It wasn't that cold, but I needed her to cover up. She took it gratefully and pulled it on. I admired her in it, under the fabric that held our insignia and our number, *43*. Somehow, she looked sexier in my hoodie than she did without it. She looked like mine. All covered up, not for anyone else but *me.* Something wicked stirred in my gut and crawled along my skin, and I couldn't help myself. I pinched the hoodie and pulled her closer. She came forward without protest, then I stopped her, our torsos inches apart. If her father knew she was here, that I touched her, he'd call off our deal. If he did that, we were fucked. I couldn't jeopardize my brothers, our plans, and our income for her. If I wanted her— *really* wanted her—I had to play the long game.

"Don't wear it outside," I muttered, releasing her. "Just to be safe."

Disappointment tore across her features, but she swallowed it well, turning her attention on our clubhouse, on the tall, black and white walls, and the club emblem that stared down enemies as they rode by and welcomed us home after a hard ride.

"My friend," she said an eternity later. "She likes this place. No idea why."

"Your friend, she a clubslut?"

Izzy grimaced. "Before tonight, I would've said no. Now? Yeah. I think she is. Do you know her? Chelsea?"

I knew Chelsea. We all knew Chelsea. She was the rich little female who showed up whenever her daddy made her mad or she was itching for a few lines of snow. That bitch pulled trains with patch members for cocaine then went to her expensive-ass fashion school, pretending she wasn't degraded and fucked in all holes at once, pretending she had a place in high society. The men loved her, but I kept my distance. I didn't trust her. I didn't trust how easily she was persuaded by drugs and money.

"Is that your subtle way of asking me if I've fucked your friend?" I asked. I could break her heart and lie, make her hate me, that'd be the smart choice, but as I watched her stomach turn in her expression, I couldn't. "She's not my type."

Isabelle arched a perfectly manicured eyebrow. "You have a type?"

I nodded. "Don't you?"

"I…" She frowned in thought. "I guess I do."

"Tell me."

She flicked her gaze the length of my body to my shoes then back up to admire my hair. "Tall, broad shouldered, dark hair, and eyes like whiskey."

"You described ninety percent of the men here," I deflected, feeling uneasy under her esteeming gaze.

"No." Izzy stepped forward and leaned, brushing her chest against me. She craned her neck and tilted her head back to look me in my eyes. "I meant *you*, James. You are my type."

James. I glanced at her mouth. My name sounded personal on her lips—*intimate* even—and my heart thundered. No one called me James, not on its own. Not anymore. It made something stupid flutter in my chest. Isabelle Laurent revered me wholeheartedly, of that I had no doubt, and I hated it. Hated how vulnerable I felt.

"You have a real pretty mouth, you know that?"

She tilted her head endearingly. "What does that mean? To have a pretty mouth?"

"It means I like the way you speak. It means I wouldn't mind kissing it." I dipped my head an inch, and she lifted onto the tips of her toes, encouraging things she had no business encouraging. "Wouldn't mind fucking it, either," I added, mostly to remind her there was no romance here.

I didn't have the capacity for romance. I was a murderer, a criminal. I was toxic, a controlling asshole in every aspect of my life, of that I was sure. I'd be a drop of noxious oil on her pure snow.

Izzy's eyes widened, and she laughed, covering her face. I felt the embarrassed heat in her blood; it seemed to wash off her in waves and lick me all over. A clubwhore wouldn't've batted an eyelid, but Izzy was used to men who didn't engage in public displays of affection, who spoke perfect English, drank their booze from crystal glasses, and only fucked in the missionary position.

"Cozy," Armi said, appearing out of nowhere.

Startled, Isabelle lowered herself from the tips of her toes and stepped back. She avoided looking at him as he sauntered past. He peered sideways at me and gave me a shake of his head, his long, blond hair pulled into its usual bitch bun.

"What're you shaking your head about?" I asked.

"Nothing." He waved me off and kept walking toward the garage where we kept our trucks. "Come on, Blondie."

She looked at me longingly, pursing her lips, her big eyes sad. With a gentle sigh, she turned in Armi's direction, and in the distance, a garage door motor churned, and metal squeaked.

Isabelle walked off, and I had every intention of letting her leave…but impulse got the better of me.

"No kiss goodbye?" I teased, and she stopped

and looked over her shoulder at me. "I gave you one the last time we met. Fair is fair."

Smirking, she angled her body toward me. "Did we kiss? I don't remember."

"Bullshit you don't remember."

I pushed off the clubhouse and stepped forward to tower over her as she shrugged her shoulders, bunching the excess fabric of the sleeves of my hoodie in her fists, protecting her hands from the cold.

"I've had a lot of kisses since then."

I growled and grabbed her, one hand at her throat, the other deep in her golden hair, and I pulled her hard against me. She didn't need to remind me she was with Pierce. I saw them—saw them kiss, saw them fuck. That preppy bastard was lucky to be alive.

"I'm gonna pretend I didn't hear that," I told her, and she scowled.

"Don't act like you've been a saint since that night. You've had your fun too."

"You're damn right I've had my fun," I admitted, squeezing her tighter. There was no point lying about it. I was certain Chelsea shared stories with Izzy about private nights at the clubhouse. "But I don't kiss them."

Isabelle didn't balk at the fact I confessed I'd had sex regularly since the night in her bedroom. Did she care? Did the thought of me inside another woman eat at her the way Pierce inside her ate at me?

"And that makes you better than me?" she asked.

"No. We have no loyalty to each other. We're

strangers."

And that was why none of this made sense. I'd lusted over a woman before, gone well out of my way to get what I wanted, but it was nothing like this. Izzy had every fiber in my being wrapped around her finger, and I felt powerless. It concerned me how far I was willing to go to get her, how deep I was contemplating betraying Judge and the club just to have her.

"Strangers? I suppose we are," she whispered, realizing that fact was true as she flicked her stare between my lips and eyes. "It's almost sad you don't kiss the women you sleep with. I loved kissing you. You're good at it."

I swallowed. "Thought you didn't remember?"

"I was teasing. How could I forget? Your kiss consumed the last year of my life."

Baby. I crushed my lips to hers, and her body tightened against me. I wanted to continue to ruin kisses for her by kissing her in a way no one could ever compare. And when her dad was finally out of office, I would slap my name on her for real and take her as my woman. I'd rip her from her empty life of luxury and bring her to my world. *My pretty pink rose forever claimed by a sea of leather and metal.*

I pushed my tongue inside her mouth, and I devoured her, tasted her, hungrier than I was that night in her room. She allowed me full control, and I fucking ran with it until my fingers were too tight in her hair, and she hissed, breaking the kiss. Isabelle panted through her kiss-swollen lips, the lower one glistening in the dim light.

"Can't you take me home?" she asked, touching me, gripping my torso and pressing her hips to mine. "We'll be alone until late tomorrow morning."

I groaned. Alone? In that big-ass house of hers? I imagined spending the night in her bed, her cotton candy-colored sheets wrapped haphazardly around us as I thrust into her. I'd ride her all night, leaving her sore and satisfied for a month. I blew air out of my cheeks and tilted my head back. *God.* She made it hard to do right by my brothers...but I had to. Whether or not I had her in the end didn't matter. The club was my life, and it always came first.

Reluctantly, I shook my head. "Can't. Judge made you off limits."

"Why?"

"Your father is mayor. The rest is club business."

"VP?"

Fuck. Isabelle pulled out of my arms as I looked to Armi, who stood awkwardly to the side, one hand stuffed into the pockets of his jeans, the other scratching at the back of his head.

"I gotta get her out of here or Prez will lose his shit."

Izzy walked away without a word, without a fucking goodbye, and strolled into the garage, not sparing me a glance. She was pissed off at me, an emotion I was used to receiving when it came to women.

"Bring my hoodie back," I ordered, turning away. "And if you tell Judge what you saw, I'll tell him Iris outshot you at the range again this week."

He swore at me, but I kept walking. I knew if I

stopped, I'd turn around, pull Blondie from his truck, put her on the back of my bike, and spend the night buried deep inside her—where she wanted me. Where I fucking wanted to be.

It was hard to walk away. I didn't know when I'd see her up close and personal again, and I didn't know if I could endure another year without kissing her soft, pretty lips.

FIVE

IZZY

I stare into the bowl of my silver spoon, watching remnants of my soup entree drip off. In its metallic surface, I see past my warped reflection, my bulbous nose and pinched lips, and focus on the clubhouse—a memory from last night. I see shiny bikes, blacked-out trucks, and the hungry flash in Creed's eyes before he kissed me within an inch of my life. *Again.* Last night was the perfect opportunity to get closure, to be with him and put the last twelve months of curiosity and "what ifs" behind me. Somehow, I left more curious and confused than ever. *After all I went through to track him down...* I grimace at the thought of Judge's eager mouth and rough hands as he gripped my body and overpowered me.

"What's the face for?" Dad asks, pulling me from my thoughts. "I thought pumpkin soup was your favorite. Did I get it wrong?"

I lift my eyes to Dad, who sits at the very other

end of the giant dining table, and ease my spoon into the hot soup, setting it down gently to lean against the rim.

"No, it is." I swallow against the nausea the rich, meaty smells of the lamb roast, our main course, stirs in me. "I guess I'm not that hungry tonight."

He surveys me with his dark, ocean-trench eyes, his brows furrowing, his thin lips quirking at the corner. My stomach turns as he leans forward, resting his elbows on the table, threading his fingers together in front of him. To the town, my father is a happy, relatable man who doesn't look a day over forty, but I know better. He's a tightly wound cynic who spends more money on hair dye than he'll ever admit and hates every inch of this town.

"I might go to bed early…" I mutter, pushing my chair back, wanting to get out of here before the questions start. "I'm tired."

When he sits at the dining table the way he currently is, it usually means an interrogation is about to start, and I'm not in the mood to answer a million and one questions.

"Staying out all night will do that to you."

I subtly inhale through my nose, filling my lungs. *He knows. I don't know how, but he does.* I clear my throat and exhale. "It was public night at the clubhouse, and Chelsea's leaving for New York, so we went out. I had two or three drinks and came home."

"That's it?"

"That's it." I feel attacked under his gaze. "I don't know why I have to explain myself to you. I'm an adult."

"You live under *my* roof."

"Because you won't let me leave."

"Because I know exactly where you'll go!" He slams his palms against the table, and I jump as cutlery clashes together. "Ewan told me all about your little...*obsession*."

Obsession? I straighten my spine and square my shoulders. Dad and I spoke briefly about the night Judge and Creed came to the house. As he tended to the small cut on my lip, he asked me if Creed touched me inappropriately. I denied everything, but I could tell he didn't believe me. The following week, I had a psychologist picking my brain, and I gave up Creed's name instantly, wanting to hear the words come from my lips to cement what happened in my reality. The thought of my psychologist, Ewan, leaking my secrets to my father makes me want to puke.

"I don't know what Ewan told you—"

"Your sessions are recorded. I've listened to them all." He sits back in his chair, his white, button-up shirt loosening on his slim torso. "Snap out of it, Isabelle. It'd be a cold day in hell before I let my only daughter screw a piece-of-shit biker."

I try hard to mask my mortification, but it cracks through, generating unbearable heat in my face. I shift my attention to my bowl of soup and thread my fingers together on my lap. Dad's chair squeals against the varnished wooden floorboards, and his shoes tap a condemning rhythm as he closes the distance between us. Without a word, he places his phone face up on the table. I flick my attention to the screen and grimace at the horrific picture of a blonde woman, covered in tattoos. Her makeup is smeared, her shoulder-length hair is a tangled mess, and her slim body is barely covered by her black lace lingerie set.

"Am I supposed to know who that is?" I ask, looking away from the screen to the surface of the oak table.

"Lolita Carmichael." Dad points his long index finger at the screen. "She's a regular at the Devil's Cartel clubhouse and was arrested earlier this week for prostitution. At the time of her arrest, she was in possession of a decent amount of cocaine *and* heroin." He flicks to the next photo—a brunette this time. "Carly Semgreen. Another Cartel whore arrested while jacked on narcotics. Both have a cute little skull tattooed on their ass."

Creed mentioned he'd been with other women. *Was he with these two?*

"So?" I demand, whipping my head to glare at him. "What does any of that have to do with me?"

"I'm showing you your future. Is this what you want? To be a drug-addicted slut who gets passed around by feral criminals for blow—"

I groan, rolling my eyes. "Don't be so dramatic."

"Dramatic?" He skims through his camera roll, and mugshot after mugshot flicks by. I recognize images of Judge, Armi, and Modo immediately. "They're murderers, Isabelle. They're killers, rapists, drug addicts, pedophiles—the lot of them."

I scoff. They didn't seem so bad to me. Judge let me go after I snuck into his room, Modo was obnoxious but manageable, and Armi didn't speak to me at all on the drive home. I'm not naïve. I know the Devil's Cartel MC are an outlaw motorcycle gang, but I don't think they're criminals for the sake of being criminals. Hardship and rivalry might've made them killers and drug users, but I'm not convinced they're rapists or pedophiles.

Dad stops scrolling, and my heart races. I flick my gaze over the image, over his broad shoulders and thick neck. I drink in Creed's breathtaking features, his short, groomed beard, and his unkempt hair. Warmth nips at my skin, kissing every pore. I look him dead in his dark, troubled eyes. I don't see him as a killer—as any of the things my father called his whole gang.

Dad blows smug air from his lips, shattering my daze. "You like this photo, don't you?"

Swallowing, I shrug my shoulders and look away from his phone screen. "He was the one in my room."

"James Creed," he confirms, and my tummy flips. "His name comes up in multiple recordings."

I twist my torso and cut my eyes at him. "Those are supposed to be confidential. If I knew you had Ewan recording—"

"If you knew, you wouldn't have opened your mouth."

"Because it's none of your business."

Dad seethes, his handsome, mature face pinches with his scowl, but like the polished politician he is, he quickly reins in his rage and addresses me with a stern voice. "James Creed is sick, Belle, and he's manipulating you for his own gain."

I pull a face. "Manipulating me? I've barely spoken to him—"

"You're the only leverage they have against me," Dad cuts in. "They exploit my love for you to get what they want, to break the law and keep control over the town."

I throw my hands and slump against my chair. "You're being paranoid."

"Paranoid?" He straightens his spine then snatches his phone off the table. "I'm being paranoid, am I?"

"That's what I said."

Dad shoves his phone in my face, and the picture on it is too close to make out. I pull my head back, craning my neck to see. When the blurry lines of the image sharpen, my stomach drops into my intestines. I glance at the naked blonde woman on a bed then hiss, slapping my father's hand away, almost knocking the phone from his hand.

"Why are you showing me *that*?" I demand, disgust and embarrassment snaking through my stomach.

"You didn't see?" He shoves the phone into my hands. "Look at it."

I try to give it back. "No."

"I said look at it!" he booms.

I growl, turning my attention to the screen. Fire burns in my cheeks at the thought of looking at something so explicit in the presence of my father, but it fades quickly when I read the name scrawled down the milky inner thigh of the exposed female.

Isabelle. My name.

I frown and hit the info button. The image was originally an attachment from a text message. *Was he sent these?* The vulnerable woman is similar to me in look, age, and stature… Dad doesn't think it's me, does he?

"That's not me," I say, and Dad scoffs.

"I know it's not you. It's Sarah Miller, a twenty-one-year-old flight attendant from Las Vegas, and one of Creed's rape victims."

Rape? Dad tears me in two with a simple sentence. My first instinct is to deny it, to argue that Creed wouldn't do something so…*wrong.* But then I remember who he is and how little I know him. I grimace as my stomach twists painfully, winding me. I place the phone face down on the table as sickness spreads through my veins, threatening to upturn the little amount of soup I ate.

"If he raped her, why isn't he in prison?"

"She refuses to speak to authorities," he replies, turning his phone onto its back. "They'll kill her if she does."

He browses his camera roll again, and a handful of women flick by, all in compromising positions, all similar to me, and all with my name on them. Guilt grinds my bones to dust, and bile rises in my throat. Disgust poisons my lust for James Creed, my desire for him turning to sticky tar in my veins.

"I don't need to see any more," I force out. "I get it—"

Glass breaks, and I whip my head to the front of the room, where eight large windows face the street. They smash, one after the other, shattered by a shower of bullets that rip apart everything in their wake. Dad shouts over the noise and grabs my shoulders, yanking me out of my chair. I squeal as he throws me to the floor and dives on top of me, shielding my body with his. I squeeze my eyes shut and cover my ears as wood, glass, and food rain down on us. Adrenaline is hot in my veins, and my lungs fail to expand under my father's weight.

"It's them," he shouts in my ear, and I assume he means the Devil's Cartel.

What do they want? Why would they do this? The deafening sound of bullets cease, but a high-pitched ringing remains, piercing my eardrums. Over it, I hear low rumbles of engines and shouts of men getting closer. I cry and tremble, a pathetic mess already surrendering to our fate. Dad can't fight them, neither can I, and Dad is an anti-gun politician. We don't own a firearm of any kind. I shudder. *Will they kill us? Will Creed kill me? Will he do to me what he did to those women in the photos?* Cursing, Dad rolls off me, kneels beside me, and pulls me up to join him.

I turn my head and gape at the damage, at the mess they've made of our otherwise immaculate dining room. It is my favorite room in the house since its large front windows showcase the sole tree in the front yard, the one my late mother used to read to me under.

"You need to run," Dad pants, cupping my face, forcing me to look at him.

I grab his forearms as pieces of glass and chunks of ceramic plates dig into my knees, embedding in my flesh. Run? Where will I go? I open my mouth to speak, but the words don't come. Where are the police?

Standing, Dad yanks me to my feet and pulls me across the floor to the hall entrance. If I run straight down it, bypass the kitchen, the maid quarters, and the storeroom, I can run into the backyard and escape into the dense forest behind our home. *Bang!* Dad roars and crashes to the floor at my feet, blood instantly soaking through the chest area of his shirt.

"Daddy!" I shriek and drop to my knees, but he swats me away, groaning in pain and gasping for air.

"Go!" he shouts, clenching his body, bringing his knees to his chest. "Run!"

I choke on a sob, but I do as I'm told. I force myself to my feet and sprint down the hall on autopilot, bile sitting in the base of my throat, ready to be unleashed the second I stop. *Where do I go? What the fuck do I do?* Before I realize it, I'm across my yard and halfway over the fence. In the distance, sirens ring, sending a mixed sliver of ease and apprehension through me. I drop over the fence and push through the shrubbery. Sticks whip and slice at my skin, and dried twigs stab into the bottoms of my bare feet, but I keep going. I keep going until the moon no longer seeps through the canopy to light my way. I keep going until I slam into a hard mass.

"Shit. Izzy?" the voice says.

Grunting, I stumble back and trip over my own feet. I fall backward and squeeze my eyes shut. I clench all the muscles in my body as I brace for impact, but it doesn't come. I'm caught by my forearm at the last second by a man with a large hand and a strong grip, a man who smells like leather and rich cologne. He tugs me upright, and I yank my arm free, squinting into the darkness.

"Don't touch me," I snap, tears stinging my eyes.

"Fucking grab her, Creed," another man orders, and I backstep away from the large shadow that towers over me, only to press my behind into the hard body of someone else.

Creed, the shadow in front, steps forward. Dry twigs snap and crunch under his heavy boots, and I hold my hands out, pressing my palms against his firm stomach. He clenches, and I push against him.

"Let me go," I plead, silent tears dripping from my nose. "I want to go."

"Where you gonna go, Blondie?" the other man asks, and I recognize his voice this time. *Damon Judge.* "Hm? Back to your house? To the cops?"

I ignore him, keeping my attention on a shadowed Creed. "James…"

He snaps forward, grips my shoulders, and jerks me toward him, crushing me against his body, restricting air to my lungs. Even so, I manage to scream. It's so loud my eardrums threaten to burst as I thrash against him.

"Jesus-fucking-Christ!" Judge booms, sandwiching me against Creed with his body.

He covers my mouth, grips my hair, and wrenches my head on an angle, causing my scalp to burn. There's a sharp pinch against my neck then a quick flush of warmth through my body, weakening my muscles. Panicked, I struggle and shout until my muscles are too fatigued to comply. Blowing air from my nose, I sag in between them and close my eyes, defeated. Lethargic.

Judge steps away, and my knees give out from underneath me. Cursing, Creed holds me tighter, wrapping his arms around me, his grasp less aggressive now. My consciousness comes and goes in waves. When I open my eyes, blurred circles greet me, and shooting pains kill my neck. I hear leaves crunching and sticks snapping under heavy boots, and my body gently bounces as I'm cradled like a baby. I try to lift my head from its hanging position over the crook of an elbow and fail.

I faintly hear a male voice crackle over a radio. "Cops have arrived."

"Update me on Jonathan," Judge says, and I groan, a distorted sob at the thought of leaving my father behind. "Dead or alive, I want to know."

"Relax, Blondie," Creed grumbles, and my lids grow heavy. "You're safe."

He bounces my unmoving body in his big arms like I weigh nothing, righting my head so it rests against his chest. My head swims with thoughts of him, made worse by his smell. The once-appealing wafts of leather, rubber, earth, and man are now unpalatable. The photos I saw earlier assault my incoherent mind. Creed fucked them all—*raped* them all. He wrote my name on their skin and sent them to my father. Safe? I'm not safe with this man—with any of them.

"I hate you," I murmur, my fingers twitching. "Don't touch me."

"What's she saying?" Judge asks as sticks and dry leaves give way to gravel under their feet.

"Don't know. Can't understand her."

I moan, and my head slides back, dropping over the edge of his arm again. A single tear runs into the curve of my eye socket, over my eyebrow, and across my forehead to absorb in my hairline. With another bounce, Creed rights my head again, and I rest my temple against his chest, against his leather vest.

I part my lips, letting out a loud rush of air. "Don't hurt me."

He holds me closer, tighter, and brushes his thumb along my thigh. Whether he heard me or not, I don't know. I guess it doesn't matter. Bad men like him do what they want, and there's not a whisper in the world that can stop them.

SIX

CREED

"What're you doing, Creed?" Judge asked, and I opened my eyes, lifting my head from the hard wall as he extended a cold beer to me. "You're gonna sit outside her door all night?"

I took it, swallowed a mouthful, then rested my forearms on my bent knees. What the fuck was I doing? Our resident doc, Harlei, said Blondie was going to be okay. Might wake up with a killer headache since Judge jabbed her with a dose of ketamine, and the blood wiped from her body exposed superficial scratches from her run through the dense forest. Other than that, she was in perfect health.

Judge lowered himself to the floor beside me and drank his beer. His movements were sluggish, his hands steady. I suspected he was a few beers deep already. It'd been a stressful day for him. Micky, one of our scouts on the western outskirts of town, reported a group of Twisted Sons entering town limits before lunch. He followed them to a truck stop we allowed other gangs and nomads to use whenever they passed through. If they ate, filled up their tanks, and left decent tips for the staff, we agreed to let them leave our turf unbothered. Micky confirmed they did just that then went on their way. Later, when asked to report what time the intruding gang exited the town, no one could tell us, so Judge and a handful of our men spent the day trying to track them down. They couldn't. It was as if the Twisted Sons disappeared off the face of the earth. We figured one of the scouts was slacking and didn't see them leave, so we belted them all, save for Micky, for not doing their jobs.

At seven-thirty p.m., Ayr reported that the cops were radioing suspect phrases to each other. They mentioned Isabelle's attendance at our open night, her pissed-off father, a group of *vengeful* bikers, and her address. It wasn't much to go off, but we headed in that direction anyway. We made Armi, Rah, and Hawk watch the front of the property while Judge and the rest of us waited in the forest behind her home, ready to breach from the back and catch the assholes who pretended to be us. At eight p.m., the "Devil's Cartel" were cited over the radio, and all on-duty police officers were ordered to arrive at the Laurent residence at eight-twenty p.m. and not a second earlier. Again, *suspect*. Not long after, the gunfire started, and calls came across the radio like rapid-fire, our club name repeated over and over. It sounded like a bad script, a fucking set up—and it was. Those Twisted Son bastards were wearing our colors, and it was only a matter of time before the cops came knocking on our door. We needed the clubhouse squeaky clean by the end of the night. Thank fuck for hang arounds and prospects.

"Any news on the mayor?" I asked Judge.

Jonathan was home when it happened, that much I knew, but his body held an unrecovered status at the moment. Blondie's did, too.

"No. No one knows where he is, whether he's dead or alive." Judge frowned. "Doesn't add up."

It didn't add up. If Jonathan Laurent wanted to frame us, why would he risk his daughter? No doubt she was under the impression we were the ones who shot up her home. She was terrified when she ran into me. Didn't want me anywhere near her. Whatever her father did or said, it changed her entire outlook on me.

"Creed!" Harlei shouted from inside Izzy's room, a large space we turned into an infirmary when our old road captain, Ryx, crashed his bike, earning his broken wings. He didn't want to go to a hospital, so Harlei did the best she could to fix him up. He succumbed to his injuries a week later, but the infirmary stayed, and Harlei worked her ass off to stock it as good as any hospital for future mishaps. "A little help?"

I left my beer on the floor, leaped to my feet, and threw open the door. My gaze flew to a terrified Isabelle, who backed herself into a corner, a pair of scissors held out in front of her, warning Harlei away. She looked terrified, her skin whiter than normal, her big, blue eyes wider. Isabelle looked at me, really looked at me, and I watched as disgust and dread twisted through her features. I frowned.

"Not a good idea, Blondie," Judge said, amused, as he entered the room behind me. "Harlei will bury you."

I glanced at Harlei, who rolled her eyes. "I was applying more antiseptic to the soles of her feet when she came to," she said, taking off her gloves to sanitize her hands by the sink. "She doesn't want me anywhere near her. The comedown from the ketamine has made her aggressive. Shouldn't last long."

Harlei tightened her messy bun of blonde and blue hair on the top of her head and smoothed her palms down the front of her tight tee as she sauntered past, smiling wickedly at Judge and me.

"Good luck," she added on her way out. "Bitch is crazy."

Harlei closed the door behind her, leaving us alone with Blondie.

"I need to speak to Harlei. You got this? Or do you need my help wrangling her?" Judge said, nudging me with his elbow.

I didn't need his help. I didn't need anyone's help handling the wild woman in front of me.

"I got it."

Laughing under his breath, he left the room. In the silence, I could've sworn I heard the rapid beat of her heart. She was scared of me—*terrified*—and I hated it. Did she really think it was us who stormed her home? That I'd bring that kind of violence to her doorstep or strike that much fear in her heart? I stepped forward, toward the bed between us. "Iz—"

"I want to go," she cut in, the scissors in her

73

hand trembling along with her voice. "Let me go."

I frowned, confused. Last night she didn't want to leave. She held her body firm against mine and asked me to take her home, to stay until morning. She felt safe with me, more than she should've.

"I want to go!" she boomed impatiently, and her voice cracked, her fear seeping onto her face.

"Where are you gonna go? Bullets ripped your house apart."

"*Your* bullets."

"No." I stepped closer, and she shimmied along the stone wall, lining herself with the door. "They weren't our bullets. We're being set up."

"Prove it."

"Can't. You're going to have to take me at my word."

Isabelle laughed once, a bitter sound. "Your word means nothing. Y-you're a criminal."

"Not a plot twist. You already know that."

She shook her head, her lips quivering, her eyes lambent with tears. "You're worse than I thought, *so* much worse."

I frowned deeper. *What the hell is she talking about?* "If you're referring to your father, we had nothing to do with it. If we were better off with Jonathan dead, he would be already."

Isabelle straightened and lowered the scissors an inch. "Is he dead?"

"I don't know. No one knows where he is."

She pondered my words for a small eternity, relief that her father might still be alive brightened her features, but it disappeared the second she focused back on my face. "If it wasn't the Devil's

Cartel, who was it?"

"That's club business. Nothing for you to worry your pretty little head about."

Isabelle stomped forward a few steps, holding the scissors out, pointing them at my face. I fought the quirk in my lips. She felt bold with the scissors in her hand, like she was in charge. I could disarm her in a second, but I let her play brave. Women outside our club life were all bark and no bite, like chihuahuas. If she were a true biker bitch, she'd have buried those scissors in my flesh already.

"Pretty?" She flicked her angry blue stare down the length of my body and back up. "You make me sick."

Irritation and confusion clashed in my stomach, and sparks flew, heating my blood. I inched closer, leaning forward until the scissors she wielded were an inch from my nose. "What the hell is your problem?"

"I want to leave."

I used the back of my hand against her wrist to push the scissors away from my face. "Too fucking bad. You're stuck here with me until this mess is sorted out."

She seethed, her jaw clenched, her perfect, white teeth bared. "You *will* let me leave."

"Or what?"

She lifted the scissors to my face again. "Or I'll cut you."

My lips quirked. I wasn't afraid of pain. "Go ahead, baby, and make it good because you won't get another chance."

Her eyebrows rose then dove into a scowl, and

she turned the scissors on her throat. "Then I'll cut myself."

"You don't have the guts."

The skin around the tip of the scissors whitened, and she hissed. A heartbeat later, a small droplet of blood rolled down the column of her throat.

My nose twitched and my nostrils flared at the sight. "You're a goddamn brat, you know that?"

"Get out of my way."

"You leave this room and you'll have all of us to deal with. They won't care if you hack your throat out."

She sidestepped and slowly shuffled toward the exit. "They won't, but you will, and I'm banking on your affection to get me out the door."

I barked out a laugh. "My affection? You *are* crazy."

Isabelle tilted her head, and I hated it was so damn endearing. "Or maybe that's your tactic. You make women feel safe, then you turn on them."

I squinted and straightened my spine. "What are you talking about?"

"I saw the photos," she said, her voice cracking, as she reached the door. "I saw what you did to those girls."

Photos? Girls? "I still don't know what the hell you're talking about."

I stared at her as she reached behind her and turned the handle, opening the door. I followed Izzy down the hall to the main room where the men, who sat around our main table, were engaged in quiet conversation. They fell silent and stared when we entered the area. In the background, Rage Against the Machine played at a low volume.

"Christ, Blondie," Modo called from his place halfway down the table. "You look like shit."

I could kill him. It hit me then, as Ayr and Armi slipped from their seats and moved toward the exit behind Isabelle, blocking it. My stomach twisted. She was talking about the photos of the women— not *girls*—I'd sent to keep her father in check. A clammy sweat formed in my palms. *Fuck.* She was never supposed to see them.

"Women," I told her, my voice quiet so only she could hear me. "They were *women*."

"Regardless," she snapped, turning the scissors on me once more. Modo whistled and laughed, enjoying the show instead of getting off his ass to help. "You disgust me, you...you...*rapist*."

I absorbed my flinch as whistles and intakes of sharp air filled the room. Jonathan told her I raped those women? *The sick bastard!* Was that why she wanted to get away? Because she thought she was in danger? That I wanted to hurt her?

"Rapist?" Armi shouted, making Isabelle whirl on her heel. "What the fuck did you do to her, VP?"

I cut my eyes at him. "I didn't do anything. She has her facts wrong."

She glared at me. "I saw the—"

I snatched the scissors out of her hand and threw them behind me. She gulped then whipped around and sprinted toward the front of the club house, where the main room gave way to the bar area, the only place the public could hang on open nights. I stormed after her, and in the other room, Iris blocked the front door with a goddamn rifle and

Kace stood between Blondie and the kitchen, blocking her exit.

"Put that thing back in the damn armory before Judge sees you," I shouted at Iris.

She batted her eyelashes. "What? I was only cleaning it."

Liar.

Kace's stare met mine as I surged forward. "Want me to grab her, VP?"

"Touch her and I'll kill you."

Kace flashed his palms and stepped aside, giving Izzy access to the kitchen. I called after her, but she ignored me and kept running. In the kitchen, Pearl, Harlei's mom, flicked her chin to the pantry then wrapped her bread and left. I turned toward the pantry and reached for the handles then stopped. The agitation in my veins demanded I rip the doors off the hinges and drag Isabelle out, kicking and screaming. I should've.

But I didn't.

IZZY

I hide next to a gigantic sack of potatoes, their earthy smell turning my empty stomach, and I stare at a small slice of Creed's shadow as he stands right outside the large, dark pantry.

"I'm guilty of a lot of shit," he snaps then blows an impatient air out of his nose. "But rape isn't one of them."

I turn my head and rest my cheek against my knee. There's so much I want to say to him, so much I want to understand, but I don't know where to start. There's no excuse good enough to justify the images he sent to intimidate my father. Of course, Dad isn't an innocent party in all this either, with his fear mongering and propaganda. He was a liar by trade, a hype man who knew how to mince words and cleverly manipulate the masses to further progress his agenda. Creed is a criminal who couldn't care less what I thought of him. He has nothing to lose to rape allegations.

"I don't owe you an explanation, Isabelle." Creed's shadow disappears then reappears. "I did what I was told to do, and I did it without remorse because it was the closest I could get to having you. Maybe that makes me sick, but...*fuck.* I didn't hurt anyone."

My head swims, pounding like mad, and I close my eyes.

When I open them, the pantry doors are wide open and Armi is standing over me, his blond hair hanging in front of his face and over his shoulders. Rock music blasts, and squeals of delight and roars of laughter flood my ears. *They're throwing a party? Really?* I sniff, lift my head, and squint up at Armi.

"Can't sleep in here all night, Blondie," he says, extending his large hand to me. "Pearl needs to make us food, and your ass is on the potatoes."

I rub my eyes. "Can I go home?"

"Home? You don't have a front door, babe. Wouldn't be safe."

I put my hand in his, and he eases me to my feet. "And I'm safe here? With the likes of you?"

"Stay in your lane and you won't get any trouble

79

from us."

I keep my attention downcast to Armi's boots as he escorts me out of the pantry and into the kitchen. Meat sizzles on a grill, and my stomach growls at the smell that filters into my nose. I look to the old woman, *Pearl*, who stands by the stovetop, turning fat steaks and eyeing me curiously. Her silver hair is piled on the top of her head, her weathered face kind but cautious.

"You eat steak?" she asks.

I glance at the chunks of meat, still red and bleeding in the center. "Is it Wagyu No Sumibiyaki?"

Armi scoffs, and Pearl thins her dark eyes as she slaps her spatula against a slab of steak, pressing it down until it sizzles and spits. "Angus."

"Oh."

"She'll eat whatever you put on her plate, Pearly." Armi releases my hand and grabs my wrist. He tugs on me, pulling me toward the door that leads to the bar and the open foyer. "What's the matter with you? You wanna get stabbed? Because that's how you get stabbed."

"What'd I say?"

"If Pearl asks if you eat something, you say yes ma'am and you fucking lick the plate clean when you're done." He shakes his head. "Ain't nobody got the patience for your pretentious sumibaki ass."

"Sumibiyaki."

Armi escorts me into the main foyer and past the bar. I drag my attention over the semi-crowded space that's been transformed into a party zone once more, complete with stripper poles and leather couches. Everyone in the room wears their leather vest and denim jeans. My nose twitches at the scent of beer, cigarettes, and marijuana, and my head thumps worse. How can they be partying right now? Creed said the club is being framed for what happened at my house. If that's true, why are they celebrating? Why doesn't anyone look concerned?

Armi drums his fingers against my wrist to the erratic beat of the music. I glance up at him then follow his line of sight across the room. Perched on a seat with a topless woman in his lap sits Creed. My breath hitches at his intense glare from over the brunette's slender, tattooed shoulder, and my stomach flips. The brunette faces him, her chest to his, her mouth on the skin under his ear. Heat spreads through my muscles and sears across my scalp, overwhelming me.

I turn my head to Armi, who scans the room, looking for someone.

"Why are we standing here?" I shout, and he hunches, lowering his ear to my mouth. "Why are we standing here?" I repeat.

Armi brushes hair away from my ear and lowers his mouth to speak. "Looking for Iris so she can take you to your room. I'll be dead meat if I take you down the hall myself."

My attention flicks to Creed of its own accord. Our eyes lock, and his glare is lethal and sharp, cutting through me like glass. I glare back. *Who the hell does he think he is?*

"Can I show you something?"

I nod, and Armi reaches into his back pocket, retrieving his phone. He enters his gallery and scrolls down a few swipes before pressing play on a video. I grimace and turn away. Pornography? I've seen enough to last me a lifetime.

"Look." Armi snags my shoulder and pulls me back. He points at the perfect, muscular ass as it clenches and releases with every thrust. "That's *me*."

"Stunning," I deadpan.

"That's Sarah Miller," he says, pointing at the blonde he grips tight in his large hands. I think on the familiar name and hear my father's voice in my head. *It's Sarah Miller, a twenty-one-year-old flight attendant from Las Vegas, and one of Creed's rape victims.* "Nice girl. Loves cocaine."

"Why are you showing me this?"

"I don't know if it proves anything, but any woman who's been through this place was here because she wanted to be. There are no rapists here, girl," Armi says, speaking directly into my ear. "Creed likes you. Don't know why, but he does, and I can tell he's really fucking bothered by your accusations. If you believe him or forgive him, go over there and let him know. If not, leave him alone and let him have his fun."

If what he's saying is true, then I owe Creed an apology for my aggression and my accusations, that much I know, but I'm not going over there, not while he's surrounded by women and Modo, of all people. Not in a million years. Shrugging out of Armi's grip, I turn toward the hall.

"Where's my room?"

SEVEN

IZZY

I don't leave my small cell-like room, not for dinner when they bang on my door, not for the soft-spoken girl they send on their behalf, not for anyone or anything. Instead, I shower in my tiny bathroom, put on the clean Lynyrd Skynyrd shirt left on my single bed, and climb under the hideous blue sheets. I don't sleep. The thumping of the music, roars of laughter, and non-stop moaning keep me awake. Eventually, the sounds die off—*well, mostly*. The moaning has melted into a low hum, and the music has reduced to a quiet thumping, like a heartbeat. I could sleep to it...if not for the plaguing thoughts of Creed. What is he doing? *Who* is he doing? I huff and roll onto my side, facing the concrete wall. It's none of my business. My house was shot up, my father too. I have more important things to focus on, like getting out of here and locating him.

Still...I can't help but pine. I don't want to be at odds with Creed, not like this.

Exhaling, I push back the thin covers and slip from the bed. The black, faded tee I'm wearing hangs loosely from my limbs, the hem brushing my thighs. In a couple steps, I'm at the door. I grab the handle and ease it down. It clicks, and the hinges squeal as I gently pull the door open. I startle, and my heart races when my gaze flicks to my apparent babysitters sitting against the black wall across from my room. I tip my head at Kace, the prospect, who sleeps soundly against a young woman, his head resting on her shoulder. They wear identical cuts of brown leather—which is peculiar. She doesn't look like a biker. She's tiny, smaller than me, and not a single tattoo inked into her softly tanned skin.

I hold my breath as I close my squealing door then quickly tip-toe toward Creed's room—the one on the right, not the left. The muffled sounds of feminine moaning grow louder and louder the closer I draw to the end of the hall, to Creed's room. My stomach ties itself in knots and jams at the base of my throat. It didn't occur to me that the passionate moans could be coming from his room. I stop at the end of the hall, Judge's room on my left, Creed's on my right. Swallowing hard, I inch toward Creed's black door and press my ear to the wood. The longer I linger, the more I realize the noises are coming from behind me, from Judge's room. I close my eyes and let out a sigh of relief. I've come to terms with the fact Creed has been with other women, but I don't know how I'd handle it happening under the same roof as me.

I push on the handle, and it moves smoothly and silently; the hinges on the door do, too. I step inside his dark, cold room and close the door behind me. My eyes quickly adjust to the dark with the help of the moonlight that pours in from the skylight above his gigantic bed. On top of the mattress, a large body lays to one side; the other side remains neat and untouched.

I head toward it, propelled only by my craving for comfort from him, and I slip under his crisp sheets that carry a gentle lavender smell, reminding me of that night in my room. He doesn't move as I slide over, my body parallel to his, our face inches apart. Our gazes meet, and to my surprise, there's no sign of sleep on his face. Even in the dim light, he looks as alert as he does in the middle of the day. I reach out and touch his hip, and he releases a gentle rush of air. I inhale his clean, soapy scent and shuffle closer, gliding my hand up the side of his body and onto his ribs. His body is firm, perfectly carved from stone, and his skin is warm and welcoming. He touches my outer thigh with his fingers first then his whole palm, gliding north. A flush of goosebumps flutter down my spine.

I should apologize to him, but I can't. I don't know how. Instead, I move my head forward, and he copies. Before I know it, our lips crash together in a heated kiss. I place my hand at the back of his neck and pull myself closer, desperate to squeeze us together, the way I've wanted us to be from the moment I saw him. Grunting, Creed grips my thigh, and I gasp as he yanks my pelvis forward, hooking my leg over his hip. I notice under my bare thigh that he is also bare. *He sleeps naked.* And there's no ignoring the effect I have on him right now. His cock is hard between my legs, pressing eagerly against the flat of my belly. A burning, tingling sensation runs through my limbs. I reach down between us and grip him. In my hand, he's hot and firm and much bigger than Pierce. I break the kiss, gliding my palm down his length to cup his balls. Everything about him is smooth, perfect, and tight. I didn't peg him as a man who cares much about his pubic hair and whether there's too much of it.

"Did you bring that woman to your bed?" I ask—no, *demand*—I *demand* to know.

"No." He reaches over my arm and pushes his hands into my panties, gliding a single finger down my center, exploring like he already owns it. "I don't bring whores to my bed. Not this bed."

A sharp pang of jealousy zaps my stomach, and heat gathers at my collar. "So you took her to another bed?"

"No." He bites my lower lip until I hiss then drags his rough finger up my slit to circle my sensitive bundle of nerves at the top. "Didn't take her anywhere. Didn't want to. I should've, after seeing you holding hands with Armi."

"I wasn't—"

"You fucking *were.*" Turning his head, he buries his face in the pillow by my ear, his lips touching my lobe. "You're lucky he's still alive, that I didn't make you watch as I wiped his face with the floor. This pussy, Isabelle…" He pushes a thick finger inside me, burying it deep, setting me alight. "Is *mine.*"

I inhale, and the breath I store feels too big for my chest, making my brain spin in my skull. No one has ever said such inappropriate things to me before. No one has claimed me like this, with such ferocity, such violence, as if he'd murder anyone who contested his claim. With Pierce, we never spoke during foreplay or sex. It just happened, and that was it, never to be discussed. Talking about sex and my desires embarrassed him, made him flush like a young girl, but not Creed. He lifts his head and stares into my eyes, my soul.

"Did you hear me?" he asks, massaging me from the inside, pressing a spot that makes me feel like my body is levitating off the mattress.

I nod, my breath hitching, my eyelids fluttering. "Yes."

"Not good enough." Creed rolls toward me, moving his body on top of mine, and my hands slip from his balls to grip his shaft once more. "Do you want to be my bitch?"

I nod again, jerking my hand up and down his impressive and intimidating length. I swipe my thumb over his thick head, collecting slippery beads of his arousal. "Y-yes."

He pulls his hand from my body, from my panties, and I descend from the euphoric madness his touch promised. He slips from my hand, and disappointment bubbles in my chest as he rears back, taking the sheets with him. Panting, I drag my stare up the sculpted length of his inked, muscular torso and rest on his face. The light from the moon is subtle, but it's enough for me to make out the rises and depressions of his sculpted body. How'd he get so big? So beefy? James Creed is more beast than man, and I'm only a helpless kitten teasing a salivating wolf. I shouldn't be here. I'm way out of my depth, but I insist on treading the water.

"Judge is gonna kill me…" he says, leaning forward to curl his thick fingers around the band of my white underwear. "He made you off limits because of our relationship with Jonathan."

"And you care what Judge says?"

"I have to." Creed tugs them down my legs and tosses them over his shoulder. "But you're here, in my bed, because Kace didn't do his damn job properly. How am I supposed to turn you away?"

I press my knees together, and Creed shoves them apart, baring me to him. I lift my back off the bed, resting on my elbows. "Do you want me to go?"

Placing his hand against my pubic bone, his fingers flat to my taut tummy, he presses his thumb to my clit and rubs it, making my abs clench. "Yes."

I balk. "Yes?"

"Yes." He leans over and kisses me, briefly flicking my tongue with his as he pushes me onto my back. "You'll go back to your room, and we'll never speak of your little visit, but first we're going to make each other come. Think you can manage that?"

I lick my lower lip and open my legs wider, hating how easily his thumb makes me slick with arousal. I reach between us and grab him by his hard cock again. "I'm not a virgin."

Does he see me as inexperienced? I suppose I am compared to him. Still, I know my way around the opposite sex. I'm ashamed to admit, even internally, that I imagined my ex-boyfriend, Pierce, as Creed in my head. Every time we were intimate, I became swept up in a fantasy, one where I took control of the man who consumed my every thought and I rocked his world.

"I know you're not, but you've never had a man like me."

And that's the truth. It was easy to please Pierce.

"How do you know?" I stroke him while he rubs me, and we release a moan at the same time, his baritone sound complementing my higher, feminine notes. "I could have."

"I mightn't've been in the picture, but I've kept tabs on you, Blondie." Creed rocks his hips, pushing my hand lower until my thumb touches his. "One boyfriend. One lover. One small cock in your tight little pussy."

He laughs under his breath, and my lips quirk. I don't think Pierce has a small penis. Average, maybe, but not small. Of course, I keep that to myself and continue to stroke him while he circles his thumb over my sensitive bundle of nerves until I can barely keep my hips on the mattress or my grip on his length firm enough. Cursing, Creed pulls my hand off him and pins my wrists above my head, the tip of his bare, firm cock pressed against my center. His grip on my wrists tightens, and he rolls his hips forward, pushing against me, sliding his hot, hard flesh along me. I moan his name in disappointment and frustration as he leans over me, watching me squirm underneath him.

"You want it bad, don't you?"

I nod, arching my back to be closer to him, and he shifts his hold, gripping both my wrists in one hand and pushing my shirt up, his rough palm gliding along my ribs to expose my breasts. He cranes his neck and envelops my hard nipple in his mouth, kissing it as if it were my mouth, licking it as if my swollen peak is my tongue. I groan, and the guttural sound I release is a needy, raspy sound I've never heard fall from my lips before, a result of his touch.

God. He's right. I've never had a man like him, and after this, I don't think I'll want anyone else.

CREED

I moved my hips, sliding my bare cock along her soaking pussy, and she writhed. In my grip, I felt the tendons in her wrists move as she balled her hands into fists and ground her hips against me, wanting more, seeking more. I wanted to be inside her. It'd be so easy to slip inside, to take her, but I wouldn't. When I finally had her, there'd be no hesitation, no guilt for betraying my club. She'd be free to be mine, and Judge would know exactly where I was, what I was doing, and who I was doing it with. They'd all know. I'd make sure they heard her, that they knew who she belonged to. I released her breast then claimed her mouth, kissing her hard while I moved on top of her. Arousal leaked from us both, making it easier to slide, and Isabelle was getting closer to her release. I could tell by the way she moved and the noises she made, so I picked up my pace, bringing myself closer and closer to spilling over the flat of her stomach.

Powerful shockwaves of pleasure exploded

through my system and bubbled at the base of my length. *I could bury myself inside her...it would be so easy.* I broke the kiss and pulled back. Keeping my grip on her wrists, I reached between us and grabbed my cock. I'd never been so hard, so fucking desperate for pussy. I jerked myself against her, burying the very tip of myself in her creases, pressing hard against her little clit. Her breath hitching, Izzy bucked her hips, pushing my cock to her entrance. My lips parted, and she pushed down on me, stretching her tight hole over the tip of my dick. For a second, I didn't think I would fit, but my hips flexed of their own accord, forcing the whole head of my cock inside her. We gasped at the same time. She was tight, almost too tight.

"Oh, fuck," she hissed, her voice cracking into a rasp. "James."

She moved her hips again, desperate to get more of me inside, but I tightened my grip on my shaft, my fist against her pussy so she couldn't pull me deeper, so I couldn't thrust deeper. I groaned and closed my eyes as she rolled her hips, squeezing the life out of me. Her breathing, shallow and quick, was all I could hear, and it stirred unbearable pleasure between my legs. She felt good. Too good. I clenched my jaw against the urge to let my pleasure erupt and pulled out of her, sighing in relief when the pressure in my balls subsided. Growling, Izzy bucked her hips, searching for me, demanding more, but I wasn't going to give it to her. Not until I could truly make her mine.

"VP!" A shout and a bang into the hall wall shattered the bubble I immersed myself in.

I tensed then shook my head. *What was I doing?* Releasing Izzy's tiny wrists, I eased away from her to get clarity. *I should wait until this is over. If I wait...having her will be sweeter.*

"Fuck, Iz," I swore, pushing my fingers through my hair. "We gotta stop."

"Stop?" She thinned her eyes then sat forward and grabbed me. I cursed as she slid onto my lap and wrapped her soft thighs around my hips, burying her fingers in my hair, grazing her mouth against mine. "I don't want to stop, not when I'm so close. Not when you make me feel so good."

Jesus. I tilted my head and glanced up at the skylight, and she pressed her lips to my neck, kissing me all over, licking me, making it hard for me to think straight. Blondie was sexy, and soft, as if she hadn't lifted anything heavier than a silver spoon her whole life, and it turned me on.

Another bang and a shout in the hall snagged my attention, followed by footsteps and a pounding fist on my door.

"Sons inbound, VP," someone shouted, and hair rose all over my body as a sick feeling twisted my stomach. *Shit.*

"Get dressed," I told her, easing her off me. Cool air clung to the parts of me she warmed, and I hated it. "Hide."

Resting on her elbows, she frowned up at me, pressing her knees together. "Hide? Why hide? What's happening?"

I left the bed and stormed to the bathroom. Adrenaline manifested in my veins, causing my heart to race. Twisted Sons are coming *here?* They had some big brass balls to approach our clubhouse after the shit they pulled. I flicked on the bathroom light, gathered clothes I'd already worn. Didn't matter if I got blood on them.

I slipped into my boots and yanked open the bathroom door. Izzy stood awkwardly beside the bed, squinting at the light pouring from the bathroom. She folded her arms across her chest, her sexy bare legs sticking out from under a shirt that wasn't mine. I cut my eyes at her and stepped forward. She swallowed hard.

"Whose fucking shirt is that?" I demanded, my voice low.

Isabelle glanced down. "It was on my bed."

"Don't care. Take it off."

"Take it off?"

I turned my back and stalked toward my wardrobe. From it, I pulled out one of my favorite t-shirts and grey sweatpants. When I turned around, irritation swirled in my gut at the sight of her still in the shirt and the way her wild, blonde hair draped over it. Rolling her eyes, Isabelle grabbed the shirt by the hem and lifted it, tugging it off over her head. My gaze fell to her perfect breasts and hardened nipples, then I brought it back to her face.

"I can't find Isabelle!" Kace shouted down the hall. "She's not in her room."

"You had *one* damn job, Kace. *One.*" I recognized Judge's furious bark instantly and tossed Blondie her new shirt. She quickly whipped it over her head. "Grab a gun. If you survive, you can look for Blondie later. Right now, we've got more important shit to worry about."

A heavy fist rapped on my door, startling Isabelle, and the hinges creaked under the pressure.

"Creed! Get your lazy ass up."

"All right!" I shouted back. "Give me a minute."

"What's going on?" Izzy asked, stepping closer, nervously wringing the other shirt in her hands.

I held out the sweatpants, and she took them gratefully, stepping into them one leg at a time. As expected, they were much too big for her. I sauntered forward and grabbed the strings, tugging them tight. She gasped and looked up at me. Worry filled her blue eyes and made her plump lower lip tremble.

"The same people who came to my house?" she asked, searching my eyes.

I nodded, tying the strings on her pants. "Yeah."

"Are they after me?"

"Doesn't matter," I told her, finalizing my knot. "They won't get you."

I stepped to the side and pointed to my open wardrobe. She eased toward it and hid inside, glancing briefly at all my tees, jeans, sweats, and who knew what else. Isabelle looked sexy in my clothes. I'd tell Judge she was safe in my room and that was where she'd stay whether he liked it or not. Whatever we had with the mayor was over. Dead, or alive, his daughter was mine.

I grabbed the handle to the wardrobe and leaned forward. "If I ever see you in another man's shirt again, God help you."

Her lips quirked, and her eyes flashed dangerously. She liked it when I was possessive, when I threatened violence—or *worse.*

"I don't believe in God."

"You'll wish you did by the time I'm finished with you."

"Are you jealous?"

Jealous? I wasn't a jealous person. "No."

"Then I suppose it doesn't matter what shirt I wear, does it?"

Isabelle took off her shirt—*my* shirt—and put the other one back on before smirking at me like a brat. She tossed my shirt to my feet. My palm twitched; so did my upper lip. We were caught in a standoff, and if I acted on the possessive feeling in my chest, if I showed her how easily she could burrow under my skin, she'd rule me. I drummed my fingers against my thigh before it became too much. I snapped and surged forward, gripping her collar in my hands.

Blondie made a choked sound in her throat as I ripped the fabric right down the middle, exposing a large sliver of her milky flesh and her bouncy breasts. When the shirt was in pieces, I got in her face, my nose nearly grazing hers. She arched a perfect eyebrow, smug.

Damn it. I am jealous.

"You play too much," I warned her, pushing the shreds of fabric off her shoulders. Isabelle remained silent—smug, but silent. I bent down and picked up my shirt, and she was smiling by the time I straightened. I stuffed the fabric against her naked chest. "Sit tight, sweetheart. I'll be right back."

I closed the wardrobe and exited my room into the brightly lit hall. Men ran by me, checking their guns and sharpening their knives.

"Catch, VP."

I turned my head toward the voice, Armi's voice, and *just* managed to catch the rifle he tossed at me. I held it in one hand and lowered the end, pointing the muzzle brake to the floor. I blew air out of my mouth. *It was too early for this shit.* Hanging his rifle from his shoulder, Armi tied back his hair and exhaled, content. He'd always felt less anxious with a weapon in his hands. He joined the Devil's Cartel after two tours in Iraq and was our shortest-running prospect. In the first week, we were ambushed on a run by a bunch of Nazis. We were outnumbered and lost two guys, but Armi shot most of them dead from wherever he was posted. He saved our asses, so we rewarded him with a beating. When he survived that, we gave him a patch and voted him our Sergeant-at-Arms.

"Get much sleep?"

I shook my head. "No. You?"

"Nope." He grinned at me. "Don't know why you gave the brunette up to me. She was quality fresh meat with a mouth like a Hoover. You missed out."

I shrugged my shoulders. He considered me palming the new brunette patchwhore off to him a gift, but it was strategy. I trusted Armi, but he was only human, and after Blondie saw the brunette on my lap, I didn't want her revenge fucking Armi. So I kept him busy.

"I didn't miss out on anything," I told him. "I got what I wanted."

Armi glanced at my door and swore, laughing under his breath. "Judge is gonna be pissed."

"I'll talk to him."

Speakers in the ceiling crackled. "Sons arriving in five, so get your asses into position."

Shit. They must be flooring it. I walked off, making my way to the front of the trashed clubhouse, and Armi fell into step beside me. "You'll talk to him?"

"That's what I said." I lifted my rifle, holding it in two hands. "Blondie's gonna be my bitch whether he likes it or not."

"And Jonathan?"

"If Jonathan's dead, he's no longer a threat. If he's alive, we're going to kill him for setting us up." I smirked at him. "Either way, his baby girl is mine now."

"Just like that?"

"Just like that."

We stepped out of the clubhouse and into the cool air, passing other members who waited patiently for the threat to arrive. It could go one of two ways. The Twisted Sons could drive by without stopping, or they could engage us. I didn't see it ending well either way. It was one thing to drive through the town on the main road. It was another thing entirely to use this road. This was our road, and no one used it but us; we made sure of that.

"You gonna make her your old lady?"

I frowned, peering sideways at Armi, who kept his attention on the front gate. I knew exactly where he was going with this conversation. *The DCMC Exeter Chapter Bylaws, section five—old ladies.* I fought a shudder.

"Fuck no."

He howled with laughter, earning glares from members whose names I could never remember and a mimic howl from Modo—*somewhere*.

"Because you know what has to be done if you want an old lady, unless you plan on making her *Mama* and sharing with the rest of us."

"Shut up, Armi."

I branched off to the left, and he went right. As I walked, I thought about the stupid bylaws I swore by when I joined the Devil's Cartel. I didn't want an old lady then. Nothing sounded worse than settling down with one pussy. Back then, I never thought I'd want anyone the way I wanted Isabelle. *I could keep her as my bitch and not concrete it*...but I'd have to make her my old lady after four years anyway or let her go. Before I could give Isabelle her own cut with my name on it, before I could claim her as mine and only mine, I had to share her with someone else. The act would create a pact between us and whoever she chose, a promise that in the event of my death, he would continue take care of her emotionally, financially, and maybe even romantically—if it panned out that way. If I wanted Blondie the way I was sure I wanted her, I'd have to come to terms with the bylaw then explain it to her too. When it came down to the wire, and Blondie wanted to choose another member, I'd heavily guide her toward Judge. I trusted him with my life. I trusted him to respect that Isabelle was mine during and afterward. And if I died, I knew he'd take care of her. He'd treat her like family, even if he had an old lady of his own.

But I didn't have to think about any of that

tonight. There were more important things to worry about—like the enemies approaching and telling Judge I disregarded his rule. I sauntered to my spot beside Judge and sniffed, peering into the darkness across the road. I reached into my back pocket and retrieved a cigarette from its pack. I always had one before moments like these, not knowing if it'd be my last.

"Where were you?" Judge asked, leaning against the gate, his right leg bent at the knee, a shotgun clenched in one hand. "You're normally the first one out when we get an alert."

"I was busy."

"Didn't see you with a whore."

I glanced at him. His jaw was tight, his eyes angry as he watched the road. I raked my teeth over my lower lip. Something told me he already knew why I was the last one out.

"Because I wasn't with one." I lit the smoke and dragged on it. "I was with Blondie."

Judge turned his head, and I felt his glare slice through my skin. Nothing in the world pissed him off more than someone breaking his rules.

"Are you stupid?" he snapped, turning his body toward me. "Jonathan's stored the photos you sent him, told Izzy you're a rapist, set us up by hiring the Twisted Sons to ambush his own daughter, and your first thought—your *first* fucking thought—is to put your DNA all over her?"

"She came into my room. What did you expect me to do?"

He pulled a face, a squinty face, that told me he was having a hard time trying to understand my train of thought. "Kick her out, Creed. *Christ.* It's not like there was a shortage of pussy around the clubhouse tonight." He pinched the bridge of his nose. "We have to keep her away. If they get her, and do what I think they're gonna do, it could ruin us."

I clenched my jaw as guilt pulverized my stomach. I hated it, but he was right. If Jonathan was alive, he could build a compelling case against me—against all of us—and we could lose Exeter.

"What is it about her, anyway?" he asked. Pulling a toothpick from his cut, he held it between his lips. "She looks like the rest of them. Why her? Why the fucking complicated one?"

I frowned. I didn't know myself, but I knew meeting her flicked a switch in me. When I told her to look at me and she did, my disarrayed life fell into a tidy deck, and every decision, every shitty life choice, made sense. She was mine—made for *me*—and I felt it in my bones. I poisoned her space that night. I was a dark, bad mass, an unkempt ball of toxicity, but she was pure, and when we kissed, I felt...*peace*. And I knew any one of us would do anything to get a few seconds of peace—Judge especially.

I shrugged my shoulders and glanced down the road and back. "She's got a nice set of tits."

Judge snorted, and in the distance, approaching bike engines rumbled.

EIGHT

IZZY

It's quiet for the longest time. My shallow breathing is all I hear until the gunfire starts.

"Oh my God," I whisper, sinking to my ass behind a row of hanging sweatpants and jeans deep inside Creed's walk-in wardrobe. "Shit."

My wild heart thrashes against my battered ribs and runs circles around my stomach, tying me up in knots. I'm in trouble. I don't know how, or why, but I'm in big trouble.

I squeeze my eyes shut and chew my thumbnail. When there's nothing left, when the skin around it stings, I move on to the other thumb. The gunfire gets louder, the sounds of smashing and crashing suddenly too close for comfort. Bad thoughts and grotesque images fill my mind—of Creed's violent death or mine if I'm found. I curse my father and whatever he was involved in for dragging me into it, too—for dragging everyone in this clubhouse into it.

Muffled shouting penetrates the wardrobe from out in the hall. I hold my breath and strain my ears. Outside, somewhere, an explosion booms, and the clubhouse trembles. I even hear Creed's rattling windows through the thin fabric of his clean, hanging clothes. *What the hell is going on out there?* The distinct sound of an opening door freezes me on the spot, causing my heart to painfully stutter. Light pours into the wardrobe from the crack underneath the door, and after sitting in complete darkness, my eyes quickly adjust.

"She in there?" someone demands from the hall.

I clamp my hand over my mouth and pull my feet closer to my ass, trying to shrink in size. I say a silent prayer that whoever has entered the room is a friend and not an enemy because I can't fight or run very fast, and I definitely don't know how to use a gun.

"Dunno," the intruder snaps, his British accent thick. "I just opened the door. Check the next room, will ya?"

My heart pounds in my ears, as loud as a bass drum, and the sounds of heavy boots on soft carpet send chills down my spine. Fine hair along arms stand on their ends as panic rises, and my fight or flight instincts kick in. I stand up and press my back against the cold wall. I think of every possible scenario and what I can do to get away. After an eternity, the light that seeps under the door is blocked by shadow, the shadow of a pair of boots. I drop my hand from my mouth and clench my clammy hands into fists at my sides. The wardrobe handle squeaks, the noise like nails on a chalkboard, and I launch forward, propelled by adrenaline. I slam into the door, and the man shouts as he stumbles back and falls on his ass. The door shoots all the way open, hits the wall, and comes flying back. I shove my palm into it, stopping it from shutting on me, and run toward the brightly lit hall, Creed's long sweatpants getting caught under my feet with every step.

As I cross the threshold, I'm hit from behind by the intruder. I scream and squeeze my eyes shut as he bulldozes me with his weight, and we both go down. On impact, I bite my tongue and my hips hit the cold, tiled floor, sending pain radiating through me. The brute lands on the left side of my body, and I shout as every organ in that vicinity pops like a balloon. The pain lasts all of a second before another shot of adrenaline spikes my blood. The man grunts and groans, swearing and cursing under his breath about his shoulder, all while keeping a weak grip on my waist. I wiggle free, pulling myself on my arms, the points of my elbows banging into the tiles.

"Danny!" he shouts, his hold slipping from my waist to the hem of my sweatpants. "Fucking help."

I don't stop. I army crawl out of my pants and force myself to my feet.

"Danny!" he shouts again, and I run.

I don't think about my destination, only that I need to get out, so I sprint out of the hall and into the main area. The sickening sound of flesh slamming into flesh, knives cutting into muscle and bone, and the smell of gunpowder is enough to slow me down. I'm in the middle of a battlefield.

Pools of blood.

Dead bodies.

"Unh!" I'm thrown forward, crashing to my hands and knees as someone shoves past me and dives into the fray. I barely lift my head when I'm grabbed underneath my bicep and pulled to my feet. I dig my heels in and thrash against the grip, but it's no use. My feet glide over the floor, through blood and glass, until I'm pulled downward behind the bar. My palms hit the floor once more, glass cutting into me. Gasping, I whip my head up as the person who dragged me crouches and opens his gun—his shotgun. I lift my stare from the gun to the *Devil's Cartel* patch on the breast of his leather vest then flick it up his long, copper beard to look into a pair of excited blue eyes. *Modo.* I rush out a relieved exhale. He's a friendly—one with a gun. I'm going to be okay. I reach out and grab his vest, pulling him close where it's safe, where I'm safe.

"How're you doin', Blondie?" He grins wide, exposing beautiful teeth—which is surprising—and pulls red tubes out of his vest pockets.

"F-fine," I say, gripping him tight as he reloads his shotgun.

When he loads the last bullet, he snaps it shut. "Wanna shoot?"

I shake my head, squeezing him harder, unable to bring myself to let go. "No, thanks."

I glance at my hands, hands that are white with the pressure of my grip. I think about letting go, but my limbs are locked to me. I want to let go—I try to—but it doesn't compute.

"No?" Arching a thick eyebrow, Modo uses his

free hand to pry my fingers off him. "Then cover your pretty little ears, baby."

I do what he says. I cover my ears and draw my knees to my chest, but it does nothing to muffle the horrific bang. He lets off a few rounds, and I grit my teeth until my jaw aches. When he's done, he crouches back down, placing the butt of his gun on the floor.

"You looking for Creed?"

I shake my head. I'd go to Creed, but something tells me he's out in front somewhere, in the thick of it all. "I'm looking for a way out."

He flicks his head. "You can get out through the kitchen. I'll cover your ass so you don't get a bullet in it."

I leap to my feet and run toward the kitchen without thought, without a thank you to Modo. As I run, bullets tear up the wall, and I shriek, shielding my head with my arms.

"Unh!" I grunt as I'm grabbed from the left and tugged behind a wall and crushed against a hard body—Judge's hard body.

I blink through hot tears and frown as he smiles down at me. "Having fun?"

Why's everyone so happy? So calm? Is this a typical Sunday night in their world? I swallow hard and nod.

"Y-yes," I say, breathless and terrified. "So much."

Judge laughs, and the whiz of a bullet zips by my ear and embeds in the wall. Cursing, Judge turns my body and shoves me forward. I squeak and stumble into the kitchen, only to be caught by someone else, the ebony woman from open night. With a roll of her eyes, she turns me again and kicks me in the ass with the sole of her hard boot. Shouting, I fly further into the kitchen, nearly faceplanting on a black stone counter.

"Get behind the counter," she demands, and I do as I'm told as Judge barrels into the kitchen, two large men hanging off him.

I went to an MMA fight at the MGM Grand in Las Vegas with my father once. This makes that look like child's play. Judge thrashes, shoving the men off him. Growling, he kicks one in the stomach, sending him flying into the woman, who pulls him into a headlock and drags him to the ground.

"Blondie!" Judge booms, and I snap my attention to him. "A little help?"

Help? I gape as Judge and the man exchange blows, both drawing closer and closer to me. I try to grip the countertop as my heart lodges in my throat at the sight of such vicious brutality and violence, and the sound of flesh pounding flesh will be seared into my brain until the day I die.

"You're by the drawer," Judge snaps, ducking a fist. "Give me a knife—fucking *anything*."

Oh. I yank open the top drawer and reach in. I shriek, barely getting my fingers out of the way, as it's kicked shut by Judge's opponent's heavy boot. Judge swears, and I'm grabbed by my hair, a tight grip that sears over my scalp, and I'm yanked off my feet. I cry out then crash to the floor. I scramble quickly, moving far away from the row as Judge and my attacker grapple. I watch them from across the kitchen, my back pressed into the corner of two cupboard doors, and my world slows down. Skin ripples, air is forced from lungs, and in my ears, their violence roars, tainting me forever. Swallowing hard, I turn and open the closest cupboard. Inside, cast iron pots and pans are stacked neatly. I grab a frying pan by the handle and slide it across the floor to Judge, who frowns as he shoves the guy back a couple steps.

"Are you serious?"

I shrug. "It's cast iron."

He bends and picks it up. With a single swipe of his strong arm, Judge hits the guy over the head, a sickening crack filling the kitchen, and he goes down. I gasp as blood spills over the tiles, dark and red, and seeps into the grout, trickling in my direction.

"Mm. Not bad." Judge spins the frying pan in his hand and smiles, wide and proud. "How're you doing, Amani?"

The woman jumps to her feet with a heavy exhale, blood smeared over her forehead and staining her lower lip. "Fine. No thanks to you."

Judge turns to face her and beams with pride at the sight of her. "You can handle your own. You don't need my help. Never have."

Amani saunters across the kitchen to stand beside Judge, both out of breath. "What now?"

"We need to get her out of here." Judge turns his back to me and leans closer to talk in her ear.

His voice is low and quiet. The only thing I hear is Creed's name, and it twists my gut. What if something's happened to him? Amani peers at me from over Judge's shoulder, and I shrink against the cupboard. At that exact moment, hollers fill the kitchen as more people enter. Judging by the look on Amani's face, they're foes, not friends. Judge drops his head back, groaning.

"If you've got a gun on you," he says, "now's the time to use it."

She shakes her head. "Dropped it."

"Fuck." Judge extends his pan to her. "Do you mind?"

She scowls and snatches the pan from him. "Lazy bastard."

Amani crosses the kitchen, and Judge gestures for me to stand up. I do as I'm told, holding on to the counter to prevent myself from collapsing. I watch, in shock, horror, and awe, as Amani rushes the two men. She fights one of them, both of them, ducking and dodging like she knows their next move before they do. They rush around the kitchen, fighting, wanting blood, and I shuffle closer to Judge where it's safe. As I hide my body behind his, Amani loses her frying pan, so Judge reaches into the top drawer and pulls out a butcher knife. He whistles once, twice, and slides the knife across the counter. One of her brutish enemies dives for it, but she kicks his hand out of the way at the last second, taking the knife for herself. With a twist of her hips, she stabs the knife into his chest then spins and grabs the other, pressing his back to her torso, her knife to his throat. His coal eyes go wide, mine do too, and she rips the knife across his throat, opening it up. Blood sprays everywhere, and tiny droplets hit my arm. The blood feels heavy—*acidic*—and I swipe my palm down my forearm, wiping it away.

Turning, Judge snags my wrist and yanks me toward the back of the kitchen. I don't register what's happening until the cool night air blasts my face and the strong smell of burning fuel assaults my senses.

"Did you hear me?" Judge demands, grabbing me by my shoulders, lowering himself so we're face to face. I shake my head. "I said Amani's gonna take you somewhere safe—"

I nod. I don't care where I go or who I go with; I just want to get out of here. Away from the violence, the smells, the blood.

"Jesus, Blondie." He squeezes me in his giant hands, as if holding me together. "You're shaking."

Am I? Judge pulls away from me and reaches for a heavy, forest green sheet. Grunting, he yanks off the thick covering, exposing a handful of grubby dirt bikes. Amani is in quick, pulling a blue dirt bike away from the stack. She throws her leg over it, starts it up, then looks at me, waiting for...*something*.

"Get on," she says, frowning.

I straighten my shoulders, worried what could happen on the back of that death trap. "I don't know how—"

I make a weird noise as Judge grabs me and lifts me with ease, like I weigh nothing, and drops me on the bike, my knees either side of the cool plastic and metal, my thighs either side of Amani's.

"Take her to the cabin." He grabs my arms and wraps them around Amani's slender waist.

"She's not holding tight enough."

"I am," I argue. "I'm holding as tight as I can."

"She's gonna come flying off once I hit the dirt track."

Cursing, Judge lifts his shirt and undoes his belt. I watch, confused, as he wraps his leather belt around my waist then loops it around Amani's belt, tethering me to her. When he's done, he taps her thigh, and she speeds off, the front wheel of the dirt bike lifting from the ground, leaving the clubhouse and the carnage behind us.

NINE

CREED

"I'm not telling you shit," the Twisted Son asshole spluttered through broken teeth and busted lips.

With a shaky inhale, he spat at Judge's feet, his blood and saliva leaving a dark, wet patch in the dirt. I lifted my foot and rested my boot on an old milk crate and stuffed my clenched fists into the pockets of my cut. Armi twisted the bloodied tip of his gold dagger into his finger and looked at me then Judge.

Judge shifted against the wall beside me, angling his head closer. "He's not gonna talk."

I glanced toward the front of the shed, at the morning light that spilled through the cracks in the heavy, twelve-foot doors. I was fucking tired—exhausted—and Blondie was gone. Judge sent her away with Amani and wouldn't tell me where. I'd get it out of him, but first I had club stuff to take care of. I swung my stare back to Armi and flicked my chin. Armi dived on the bald biker we had chained to a steel chair, and I watched, unbothered, as Armi hacked his left ear off. The biker screamed until his voice box sounded like it bled. Flesh snapped apart, like elastic, and Armi threw his useless ear to the floor. Across the space, Stoic retched and turned his head, his long, brown hair falling into his face.

"Christ," he whispered under his breath, and Judge snickered. Of all of us, Stoic had the weakest stomach. Funny, given the state he left his brother in all those years ago.

"String him up by the ankles," Judge ordered, his deep voice echoing through the old shed. "Take his eyelids, nose, lips. Take him apart, one piece at a time, until he tells us what we want to know. If he still refuses, gut him like a pig. We'll get our answers elsewhere."

Judge pushed off the wall and headed toward the front doors. I followed, squinting as I stepped into the bright morning light, and let the metal door slam shut behind us.

"The answer's no, Creed. I'm not telling you where she is."

"Why the fuck not?"

"You know why."

"Judge—"

He whirled on his heel, stopping me in my tracks, pinning me with a glare. "Until I get confirmation, our arrangement with Jonathan stands, and you will stay the hell away from Isabelle."

I ran through all the places Judge could've sent

her in my head. Some places were too far, others too close. Satisfied with my silence, Judge turned his back and marched toward the clubhouse, passing by a line of old dirt bikes, the tattered blue cover thrown to the side. I tilted my head and counted the bikes. Immediately, I realized Ayr's blue bike was missing from the lot, and it all clicked.

"The cabin," I stated and watched as Judge stopped and his posture shifted as he straightened his spine and squared his shoulders, giving me the answer. "That's where you've sent her."

He tilted his head, and his torso dipped with an impatient exhale before continuing his walk toward the clubhouse. I was surprised he sent her there, to the place he built for him and his daughter before she was murdered by her mother's piece of shit boyfriend—*dead* boyfriend now. I knew how to get there. I could leave right now, and there wasn't a thing he could do to stop me.

"Get the cunt in the shed to speak," Judge called over his shoulder. "And I'll give you two days with Blondie."

I turned toward the shed, ready to take over the show. I rolled the sleeves of my hoodie to my elbows and adjusted my leather cut. I knew Judge was watching me. I could feel his gaze burning holes in my back. Hopefully, he saw I really wanted it, the two days alone with Izzy to figure out what I wanted from her. To get it, I'd make the fucker speak, even if it took all day.

IZZY

I roll over on the large bed, blow out an exhale, and stare up at the high ceiling of the stuffy cabin. On the outside, the place doesn't look like much—it's old and weathered—but on the inside, beautiful hand-carved pieces of furniture were preserved in mint condition underneath thick sheets of plastic. I know this place belongs to someone in the Devil's Cartel, but Amani didn't tell me who. She's barely spoken to me since we arrived.

I kick off the heavy blankets that, surprisingly, have a pleasant jasmine scent to them, and I stretch my sore legs. Outside, a muffled rumble shatters the late afternoon silence, and I frown. *Is Amani leaving?* Panic stirs at the thought. I slip from the bed and cross the spacious room to the door. As I brush my fingers over the brass handle, I hear heavy footsteps, the kind that accompany a robust male. My heart stutters, and I step back, putting distance between me and the door. I glance around the room in search of a hiding place then pause. Maybe I'm being silly. No one who wants to hurt me knows I'm out here in the middle of nowhere, surrounded by wilderness. I inch toward the door and take the handle in my hand. At the other end of the cabin, I hear the front door close, then a thump sounds and vibrates the varnished floorboards under my feet. More heavy steps cause excitement to sprout through the cracks of my trepidation as thoughts of Creed slip to the front of my mind.

I push on the handle and slowly open the door. The rumbling sounds of Amani's motorbike grow louder the further down the hall I tiptoe, then they begin to fade the further they move away from the isolated cabin. I pause in my mission to get to the front door and listen as keys are fumbled and dropped onto the floor—or a counter—followed by the distinct sound of a man clearing his throat. Hair prickles over the back of my neck and down my spine. I glance at my bare legs, the tops of my thighs covered by an old, red shirt I found in the drawer of the master bedroom since the one Creed gave me has blood on it.

I flick my attention to the left partition of the hall as the shadow of a broad man stretches across it. I clench my fists and hold my breath, eagerly anticipating Creed's appearance more than I've anticipated anything in my life. He steps into the hall and freezes, arching an eyebrow as he drops his stare to my bare legs. My lips part as a pang of surprise slams into my gut. The man standing before me isn't Creed at all, and disappointment leaves me aching all over. I flick my gaze over his cropped, jet black hair, blue eyes, strong jaw, and the tattoos that start under his chin and cover every inch of his throat.

"You look…" He locks his stare with mine. "Comfortable."

I swallow hard. "I am."

Turning, he flicks his head for me to follow him and peers at me over his shoulder, his gaze dropping to my legs and back. "Want a beer?"

I nod, even though I hate the taste of it, and Judge leaves the hall. I stay rooted on the spot, not sure if I want to sit and drink with Judge without pants on, when the front door is opened again.

"Might wanna bring her some pants," I hear Judge call out, and the thought of the whole club being out there is enough to send me scurrying to my room as heat blasts my face.

I pace for a small eternity before the door opens without a knock. I gasp and grab a black, square cushion from the bed and shield myself with it as Creed crosses the threshold. I glance at the plastic bags he clenches in each hand, then I'm swept up in the flash of his whiskey glare as we make eye contact. I don't know how he does it, but he makes my clothes feel like sandpaper against my skin. He makes me want them off. Creed kicks the door shut behind him, sealing us in the room. He drops the bags, and they fall to the floor without a thud, spilling clothes in all sorts of feminine hues, the tags still attached. *So much color. Did he go shopping for me?* I'm surprised by the lack of black, denim, and leather.

"You're still alive," I say, my voice pathetically weak.

"You sound disappointed." He shrugs out of his leather vest and tosses it onto the messy bed. He looks pissed—*jealous*—and I can't help the ghost of a smile it brings to my lips.

"I'm not."

"Come here and prove it."

Creed grips the hem of his shirt and pulls it over his torso and his head. His physique takes my breath away. It's not the body of a lean man, a man who lives in tight dress shirts made of the finest fabrics. It's the physique of a hardworking man, one who's pushed his body to the brink over and over again. I admire his tattoos, the skulls and thorns, roses and bones. In this light, I can tell his torso is heavily scarred, but he's had them covered with intricate swirls of ink. I bet he has a lot of stories; men from my world have no stories, no tales of near-death experiences. At least, not interesting ones.

I close the distance between us until the tips of my bare toes kiss the ends of his black boots.

"Why is Judge here?" I ask as Creed takes the cushion from my hands and tosses it across the room.

"To relieve Amani. She'd rather be at the clubhouse."

"Why are you here?"

He pinches the hem of my shirt and lifts it. I go with it, allowing him to pull my shirt over my head and throw it to the side. Blush swirls in my chest and travels north as his expression turns hungry at the sight of my naked breasts.

"Because I'd go mad knowing my best friend was alone in a cabin with my woman."

"Your woman?"

Creed grabs me, and I gasp as he lifts me into his arms, one hand pressed between my shoulders, the other against my ass.

"You're not mine?" he asks, his golden eyes flicking between mine, a mix of worry and frustration swirling through them.

I take a beat to think, knowing men like Creed value words and promises. If I were to be his, will he rule my life? Will it be any different from living under my father's thumb? Am I throwing one shitty

117

life away for another? As president, would Judge get a say on my life, too?

"What does it mean to be yours?" I ask, pushing my fingers through his hair. "Are there prerequisites?"

His lips twitch with the beginnings of a smile. "Only one that's important." He moves us toward the large bed and slowly lowers me down, pinning me with his slim hips. "Respect me."

"Okay."

He cups my breasts in his warm, giant hands and massages them, keeping his eyes on mine even as my soft, pliable flesh spills between his thick fingers.

"Respect me and I'll keep you fed and safe." He licks my nipple, dragging the pink flat of his tongue over my hardened peak, making me shiver. "And well-fucked."

I part my lips as he squeezes me tight and presses his mouth to my chest, not letting a sliver of skin go unkissed.

"We barely know each other. Doesn't that bother you?"

"I know more about you than any woman I've been with...so, no. It doesn't bother me." Creed lowers his body to press his hard stomach against mine. "I wanted you the second I saw you in that sexy, honey-colored dress."

"Outside the convenience store?"

He smiles. "I looked up as you walked by. You were the prettiest thing I'd ever seen. Judge told me you were beautiful, but seeing you with my own eyes..." He slips his tongue out to moisten his lower lip. "I knew you were the mayor's daughter, that I could never have you, so I never considered the possibility. Until you asked me to take you with me that night in your room."

I nod. I remember feeling lost and alone. Dad wanted things for me I didn't want for myself; Pierce was adamant about discussing plans for our future, his dream wedding, his dream house, and me bearing five children I didn't want. To top it off, Chelsea, who I'd been joined at the hip to since kindergarten, revealed her plans to move to the city when she finished her studies. I felt like I was drowning, then Creed waltzed into my room, a breath of fresh air, his presence like popping candy in my blood, and he tore a hole in my schedule, in my mind-numbing routine.

"Do you still want that?" he asks, and I frown.

I think about the pain in my thighs, feet, and lungs as a result of all the running and screaming. In the last twenty-four hours, I've been shot at, chased, attacked, and driven on the back of an old dirt bike at ridiculous speeds. I want Creed, and I want to be a part of his world but…

"I'm not cut out for it," I admit, and the disappointment I feel comes through in my tone. "The parties, the fighting, the violence. I'm not like Amani; I can't defend myself."

Creed takes my face in his hands and stares into my eyes, into my soul. "If I do my job right, you won't have to."

"And what about people?"

"What people?"

"The town's people. We can never go out

because they'll stare and gossip. They'll tear my father's legacy to shreds."

"I don't give a shit what happens to Jonathan or his legacy, but I promise you, no one will look twice in your direction in fear of seeing my shadow."

He'll protect me so fiercely? The daughter of the man who wants nothing more than to see him and his club behind bars? I'd be skeptical if there wasn't such a needy gleam in his eyes. Logically, I should chalk our connection up to lust, not affection, but…every cell in my being screams there's more to our relationship than rebellion or the forbidden. There's a mutual fondness I believe has every chance of growing into love. Even if it doesn't, I don't think I'd regret time spent with James Creed.

I touch his broad shoulders then glide my hands up his neck to his soft, clean hair. I haven't wanted anything as much as I want this man. Swallowing, I lift my head off the mattress and kiss his lips. He groans and kisses me back with vigor, and my body floods with heat hot enough to rival the sun. My limbs tremble with fear, knowing I'm way out of my depth with a man like him. He's nothing like the boys I grew up with or like Pierce who, in this instance, I akin to a skinny match that offered the tiniest flicker of heat that faded quickly. Creed is a sun, scorching, unyielding, and mesmerizing. Nothing in this world can extinguish the heat he ignites in my blood.

Creed takes charge, trailing kisses from my lips to my jaw, to my neck, then to my collarbone. I close my eyes and drop my head against the mattress as he continues his descent, kissing and licking me as if I'm a melting ice cream he doesn't want to waste.

He moves quickly, skillfully, removing my panties without pause in his routine, and it's impressive. My breath hitches as he kisses the inside of my thighs, drawing nearer to their apex. Of their own accord, my muscles clench and shiver with every brush of his rough beard.

"Tell me you've thought about this as much as I have?" he asks, his warm breath hitting my center.

I keep my eyes closed, afraid I'll open them and this'll all be a dream.

"I have," I say on exhale, gently flexing my hips.

Heat swirls in my cheeks, and I open my eyes and lift my head to peer at him, at his full lips, as he moistens them an inch from my most intimate part.

"I've never done this in daylight before..." I confess, suddenly nervous about all my insecurities—the extra softness around my backside, hips, and stomach and the shiny stretch marks on my hips and breasts.

"No?" He flicks his hungry gaze over my body, and I shift uncomfortably. "Such a waste. You're perfect, you know?"

Creed rakes his grateful, lust-filled stare over me again, not settling on areas I think are gross or unflattering, not for a second, and I believe him. I believe he thinks I'm perfect, imperfections and all.

I smile at him, and he lowers his head, kissing the crease between my thigh and my pelvis, forcing my breath to hitch. Then he floats his mouth across my opening, his warm breath blowing against me. I

121

tense, nervously awaiting his smooth, wet tongue to touch me, to lick me and make me feel good. A small eternity later, he presses his mouth against me, pushing his tongue through my creases, immediately finding my clit. I gasp and lift onto my elbows to get a better look at what he's doing to me. Our gazes lock, and Creed groans heartily, sending powerful bolts of pleasure through my belly and a tingling over my scalp.

"Oh," I moan, letting my head loll back as I arch against his mouth. "Yes."

"Damn. You taste good, baby."

He licks and sucks me harder, dancing his fingers against my thigh before pressing a single, thick digit to my opening. With a gentle push, he penetrates me, and the skin behind my ears pull tight, shooting fireworks down the back of my neck to sparkle in my chest, hardening my nipples to their maximum point. He licks me up and down, a delightful pace between fast and slow. The pulse he stirs between my legs throbs mercilessly, and warmth floods me as I grow wetter and wetter, allowing him to insert a second finger. Groaning, I shift my hips to get away from the pleasure he's giving, away from the unbearable sensations that build quicker than ever before.

He pulls his mouth from me and bites the inside of my thigh.

"Ouch!" I squeal and swat at him. *Ass.*

"Where're you going?"

Where am I going? I don't know. Away from his sinfully good tongue and fingers, before I let them brand me forever. "James…"

Smirking, he plants a heavy hand on my clenched stomach, holding me immobile against the king mattress while he tortures me with his skillful tongue again. He moves his fingers inside me, massaging, making my breasts sway back and forth. Following last night, it doesn't take long for Creed to build up my pleasure and dangle me over the precipice of ecstasy. He holds me there, teasing and taunting, until I'm gripping his hair and grinding my hips, seeking more pressure, more friction. Something wicked flashes in the depths of his eyes, and he lifts his hand from my stomach to grip me behind my knee and push it toward my chest. *Jesus.* He catches my clit between his lips and tugs on it. I gasp and jolt at the foreign pleasure that explodes from his rough treatment, feeling the tingling build. Creed releases my clit and does it again, and again, until every muscle in my body coils so tight it burns. I crunch my body, my breath coming out in uneven gasps as my orgasm crests, then explodes, spreading through my pelvis, through my stomach, and down to my feet.

"Ah," I moan, and grip Creed's wrist in one hand and cover my mouth with the other. "Shit."

I try to muffle the noises I make, all while Creed makes a show of what he's doing, pulling back enough to show me the length of his tongue and the tip of it as he flicks it over my sensitive bundle of nerves while plunging his fingers in and out of me. It's the sexiest thing I've ever seen—*he's* the sexiest thing I've ever seen.

My legs spasm together, my toes curling painfully until I can't stand it. I throw my head back with a growl and push against Creed's head, silently begging for him to release my throbbing bundle of nerves. Laughing under his breath, he releases me, and as if being released from a spell, my muscles unclench, leaving me a boneless mess. I turn my head and drape my hand against my chest, feeling my heart as it batters my ribs. Creed rises up and crawls over me, planting one hand beside my head to hold himself up. The other, he slides against the side of my face, turning my head with his palm to look me in the eyes. I blow out a sigh then wrap my arms around his neck and pull him down on me. His hard body hits mine and presses me into the mattress. He's heavy, so heavy my lungs can't expand the whole way as I try to breathe in his fresh, soapy scent. I don't mind it. It makes me feel secure and protected.

"Take off your pants," I demand, licking his lower lip, shivering at the feel of his denim jeans rubbing the inside of my bare thighs. "I want you. I want you to give it to me."

Creed rears back, and I follow his giant hands with my hooded gaze as he unbuckles his belt. I'm way out of my depth here with him, and I know better than to jump into sex with this gorgeous man, but I've never felt desire so strong before. My body is ready for him. I need to have James Creed once and for all.

He drags the zipper of his dark jeans down, the metal slider clicking against the teeth, building anticipation in my gut, and lets out a sigh of relief as he pushes his jeans down, letting his erection go free. I lick my lower lip as he palms himself, stroking his hand up and down his length before leaning over me. Creed envelops my nipple in his hot mouth and caresses the inside of my thigh, tickling me, forcing me to open my legs wider. He lowers his hips as I lift mine and pulls at one of my knees, opening me up so the tip of his cock presses against my entrance.

"Are you going to hurt me?" I whisper, the women from those photos flashing to my mind.

James lifts his head, hovering it over my face. He turned the women's skin red; he ruined their mascara and made their hair a tangled mess. I've never been treated in such a rough way.

"You're not them," he says then shoves into me without ceremony, burying himself completely and making me shout. "But yes, I'm gonna hurt you." He pulls back and thrusts again, grunting as he forces his entire length inside and holds still. "Because I know how much you like it."

My lips part with a shaky breath, and I feel myself begin to leak around him, a result of his passionate assault. Our gazes meet, his no longer a blazing gold, but a midnight black—an enthralling, arousing, and terrifying midnight black. It sends fire burning through my veins. I've been lusted over by many men, but the way James looks at me is incomparable.

"I do like it," I tell him, taking his wrist and moving his hand to my throat. "I like it when you're rough with me. No one is ever rough with me."

Creed tightens his grip. "Because you're Exeter's sweetheart."

"Not anymore."

He smirks, tilting his head as he cranes it. "Not anymore," he repeats, squeezing my throat until my eyes water. "You're my woman now. My naughty girl."

"Yours," I squeeze out.

He kisses me hard, filling my mouth with his tongue, then he pulls back and watches my face as he slams his hips into mine, filling me to capacity. I wince and open my mouth, but no sound comes out as he squeezes my throat in his giant hand. The fact he can crush my windpipe in an instant isn't lost on me. In fact, it turns me on more.

"Too much?" he asks, smirking.

I try to tell him it *is* too much, and I like it, but his hold is too tight, restricting my voice. I swear I feel my pupils flare, and it resonates with him as his smirk morphs into a grin.

He slams me over and over again, and my head reels. I can't breathe. Can't move. I've never felt so dominated in my life, like I'm nothing but an easy screw. Creed releases my throat, and I gasp for air, wrapping my legs around him, pulling him deeper, wanting him deeper.

"More," I whisper, breaking the kiss to move my face into the crook of his neck.

"More?" he groans, nipping my ear between his teeth, and all I can do is nod. "So greedy," he teases. "What am I going to do with you, huh?"

Creed slides a large hand under my ass and angles my hips. My core twists as he fucks with increased speed and aggression, and each thrust sends powerful surges through me. I feel alive.

Alive and blissful.

Low moans seep from my lips, moans I've never heard before, and as heat pools in my lower belly, Creed pulls out and away from me. I barely have time to voice my complaint before he's behind me, his body pressed against mine, his hand under my knee, lifting my thigh. He slams into me, and I cry out, the sweet pain of him pushing inside me radiating through my body, rippling through my muscles like a stone dropped in water.

Creed thrusts harder, and sounds of flesh slapping flesh dominates the room. I pull my knees higher and curve my back, wanting more. He releases my leg and grabs my throat, pulling me back against him, his forearm between my breasts. My breathing shakes.

"Against me," he pants, kissing me behind the ear as I reach behind me, pressing my hand to his hip, feeling his powerful thrusts as he hits me over and over. "I want you against me."

My pussy clenches around his cock, loving everything he gives me, every inch, every thrust. His name falls as a whisper from my lips, and he glides his hand from my neck to my cheek and turns my head. The muscles in my neck ache on the unnatural angle, but it doesn't deter me from pressing my mouth to his. I kiss him, long and slow, and his thrusting follows suit, turning from powerful thrusts to passionate, deep strokes. As I kiss him, he trails his fingers down my stomach and between my legs to rub my clit. In seconds, I get close, my whole body gearing up to burst, and I'm unable to control my hips that swivel of their own accord.

"I'm coming," I rasp, breaking the kiss to look down where his fingers play me. "Yes…fuck."

My orgasm takes over, and I hunch forward, my abdominals clenching painfully tight, my thighs seizing up. Warmth spreads through me as I explode into a million tiny pieces, crying out.

I move harder, faster, grinding out my orgasm until Creed releases my clit, grabs my ass, and tries to push me away from him. Caught up in the heat of the moment, I keep my grip on his hip, desperately wanting him to spill inside me since, unbeknownst to anyone, I have a birth control implant in my arm.

"Come inside me," I beg, digging my nails into his flesh, making him hiss.

"Shit," Creed growls, though he continues to push deep. "Fuck, Izzy."

Then he groans and shoves deep one last time. Stilling, I feel him spill inside me, his taut muscles spasming with every spit of his release. I rock against him, prolonging his orgasm until he clamps a hand on my hips, holding me still.

We lay in silence, the damp sweat on our bodies drying. Creed softens inside me, and the ache in my muscles comes back with a vengeance. When the fog clears, I glance down at his hand on my hip and notice the blue-black bruising around his knuckles. Frowning, I graze the tips of my fingers against them, and he twitches.

"Do I want to know what happened to the person on the receiving end of these?" I ask, my voice husky.

Creed nuzzles into my hair and kisses my neck. "Even if you did, I couldn't tell you."

"Club stuff?"

"Yeah, babe. Club stuff."

He rolls away from me and swings his legs over the side of the bed. I fall onto my back and watch as he kicks his crumpled jeans off and stalks around the bed, stomping toward the bathroom.

"Does it have something to do with my father?" I ask, rolling back onto my side, and Creed pauses at the threshold to the bathroom. "Have you...have you hurt him?"

Something aches in my chest at the thought of Dad being hurt by someone so much bigger than him. My father fights his battles with brain, not brawn. Creed would decimate him.

Straightening his shoulders, he turns around and pins me with an irritated look. I swallow hard, dreading his response all while keeping my attention above his belly button.

"Do you love him?"

"My dad?" I frown. "Of course I do."

Although we have a turbulent relationship, and I'd rather live countries away from him, he's still my father. Loving him despite his flaws is the burden I carry as his daughter. Creed's golden eyes flash with annoyance, and he purses his lips, choosing his next words carefully.

"He loves his job more than he loves you."

My eyelids flutter. "Unfortunately."

I've known Dad to be a workaholic my whole life, so Creed's statement isn't groundbreaking. I've sacrificed a lot in the name of politics, for the sake of his campaigns. Still, silent words I've thought only to myself are painful to hear aloud. I shift on the bed, suddenly coveting a shower to clean myself with.

"At risk to myself, I'll tell you that Jonathan paid a rival gang to ransack your house, kidnap, rape, and beat you—"

"That's ridiculous."

"—to keep his campaign promise to get rid of us."

"You're lying," I snap, shifting on the bed, uncaring if I leave residues of the mess we made during sex. "He wouldn't—"

"We caught one of the imposters during the fight this morning." He flashes me his knuckles. "Judge told me if I made him talk, I'd get you, so I made him fucking talk."

"Then *he's* lying."

"Doomed men have no reason to lie."

I swallow. Did he just confess to murder? A chilling swirl of dread curls through my chest then turns hot in the pit of my stomach. "You killed him? The man?"

He doesn't flinch at my question, doesn't flush, doesn't twitch. He keeps eye contact and blinks softly. "There are conversations we can have and conversations we can't have. This is the latter." Creed flicks his head toward the bathroom. "Let me clean you, then I'll cook you some food."

I stare after him as his confession about Dad sinks in. Is it true? Can I trust Creed to tell me the truth? Or is he using me against my father, like he did with the photographs? What could be more victorious to the Devil's Cartel than having the mayor's daughter as a whore on the arm of a patch member? Sickness twists through me, wringing my bones, at the thought of being played.

"Blondie," Creed calls, and I startle as his voice echoes through the room. "Shower's hot."

My thoughts spiral out of control, but I force them to the back of my mind and saunter into the small bathroom. Steam clings to the glass walls of the shower already, and Creed pushes the door open, exposing his wet, naked body to me. My lips part as I inhale deeply, and I rub my palms with my fingers. The sight of him…it stokes my blood into fire. Water drips from the tips of his wet, messy hair, and I follow them as they make their way over his sculpted, tattooed chest and into the depressions between his perfect abs. One drop trails the edge of a vein that starts in his Adonis belt and leads to his impressive cock. The water defines his beautifully sculpted body. I once told my psychologist I thought it was the leather that made James Creed irresistible to me, teamed with dark denims and faded tees. Turns out he's just as irresistible when he's naked too.

Clearing my throat, I drop my gaze to the floor and enter the shower. It's a small shower, at least a quarter of the size of the one I have at home. My nipples harden and touch Creed's flesh when the hot jets of water hit my back.

"You think I'm lying to you," he states, his voice cool and calm, and I lift my head to look him in the eyes.

"Are you?"

He glides his hands over my water slick body and pulls me close. Steam dampens the edges of my hair and fills my lungs as Creed steals the air from it. "Don't know how to prove I'm not lying, so my answer doesn't matter."

Our torsos touch, and he cranes his neck, lowering his head to kiss my lips.

"I need to see my father," I blurt out, pulling away before giving him the power to distract and silence me. "If what you're saying is true, I want to confront him."

Creed glances between my eyes, his expression not betraying his thoughts. He leans in for a kiss again and speaks against my mouth, his top lip brushing mine. "Then I'll take you to him."

"Oh." I let out an exhale. *I didn't expect that to be so easy.* "Thank you."

He cups my face and kisses me. It's passionate and demanding, and it sends my head reeling, making it hard to tell which way is up. I've never had a kiss full of lies before, but if this is it, I'm in big trouble.

TEN

CREED

I couldn't take my eyes off Isabelle as she sat cross-legged on the old daybed I helped Judge carve out of redwood a lifetime ago. She shifted underneath the gray faux-fur blanket that was draped over her shoulders and smiled politely at Judge. I listened to the way she spoke and interacted with him. She was articulate and charming, and it interested me the way she directed the conversation, always turning it away from herself, making it about Judge, who didn't notice their entire conversation was on her terms. It was a coping mechanism, a survival tactic she used to navigate vile, political waters, I'd bet.

I lifted my beer and swallowed a mouthful as I shifted in my hand-carved redwood chair and turned my attention to the center of the stone courtyard. Fire crackled in its decorative metal bowl, casting long shadows all around us. Out of everything Judge built here for his daughter, Nila, the fire pit was her favorite. Like her father, she was a little pyromaniac. Most little girls dreamed of ballerinas and unicorns, but Nila was obsessed with fire and brimstone, with motorcycles and things that went bang. She swore she'd become Queen-President and take over the Exeter chapter, and I believed her, too. She was too fucking precious for this messed-up world, and the death we brought to the piece of shit that murdered her was too fucking nice...

...even if we did keep him alive for months and slowly pick him apart until his body couldn't take any more.

Blondie's melodic laugh pulled me from my thoughts and vanquished the images of Nila's limp body as Judge clenched her tight, sobbing into the crook of her tiny neck.

"Is that true, James?" Iz asked, and I paused.

James. I love it when she calls me James. I'd been with a lot of women, more than I cared to count or cared to remember, but Isabelle was different. If anyone else, any clubwhore, called me James, I'd lose the plot, but I liked it when Isabelle called me by my first name. It was...intimate. Izzy was sincere. She wasn't trying to seduce me for my patch or my rank.

"Is what true?" I asked, tilting my head.

I'd been zoning in and out of their conversation for well over an hour. I wanted to join, but I couldn't seem to deter my mind from dark shit or getting between Izzy's thighs again.

"That you dumped fifty pythons into Modo's room through the hatch of his skylight?"

Judge snorted, and my lips kicked up at the

corner as I recalled that one morning last year and Modo's shrill squeal. "Yeah. I forgot about that."

We laughed, and it was fucking nice. I hadn't felt so unwound in years, so relaxed, so satisfied. There were still a shitload of problems to sort out back at the clubhouse, but I chose to ignore them. I was celebrating because Izzy was finally mine, and I'd take her to her father and make him prove it. His daughter was my bitch—my *lady*—and he'd see her on the back of my bike whenever we crossed paths in town, provided he didn't go to jail for what he'd done.

The urge to touch her prickled down my spine and arms. I didn't want to sit across the fire from her and barely hear her laughter over the crackle of flames any longer. I wanted to sit behind her, and I wanted to feel every laugh vibrate through her back and into my chest. I placed my unfinished beer on the ground, lifted myself out of my chair, and sauntered around the pit. She followed me with her pretty stare, smiling as I took the blanket off her and slipped onto the daybed behind her. After sex, and after the shower, she was awkward. I could tell she wasn't sure where we stood once I'd gotten what I wanted from her. To be honest, I didn't know, either. I was used to losing interest once sex was over, but it had been hours and I still wanted her as much as I did earlier.

I placed my legs on either side of her as she uncrossed them and leaned against me as I rested on the plastic-covered cushions behind me. I draped the blanket over our legs and wrapped my arms around her waist, holding her to me. She smelled good, like soap and berry shampoo, and she looked cute as hell in an over-sized white sweater with loose sweatpants. All I could think about was peeling them off her and licking her all over.

I glanced at Judge, who flicked his curious stare over us, over my hands as I held her.

"An hour alone together and you two are a thing now?" He smirked, tilted his head, and kissed his teeth, lifting his beer toward his mouth. "I guess the sex was good."

"Sex?" Izzy balked, but Judge wasn't having it.

He flicked his hand at her and rolled his eyes as he swallowed a mouthful. "Don't play dumb. I heard you. The whole fucking forest heard you."

Isabelle's body vibrated with embarrassed laughter as she shielded her face and dropped her head against my chest. I squeezed her and stroked her sides with my thumbs. She had nothing to be embarrassed about. It was second nature for Judge and me to taunt each other, and we were comfortable discussing anything at the dinner table. Hell, we were comfortable *doing* anything at the dinner table, no matter how many brothers were present. She'd grow accustomed to it eventually.

"Anyway," she deflected, pushing her long blonde hair out of her face. "We were discussing your gang."

"I hate the word gang," Judge said, sitting forward. He reached into his cooler and pulled out a can of beer. "It carries a negative connotation."

Isabelle's head twitched. Bet she didn't know an uneducated criminal could use words like that in a sentence—and correctly, too. Judge wasn't an idiot.

None of us were, except Modo.

He lifted himself out of his seat and brought it over to Izzy, who shook her head, so he offered it to me. I took it and cracked it open.

"We're good people. Have never hurt anyone who didn't deserve it. Yeah, we do bad shit to get paid sometimes, but we protect what's ours, and we support our community more than Jonathan ever has." He dropped himself into his seat and sank into it.

"You support the community, how?" Iz asked, leaning forward.

I knew Isabelle spent a lot of time helping her father organize fundraisers and charity balls, and I knew she enjoyed it wholeheartedly.

"We host blood drives and bake sales to fund cancer treatment for sick kids. Every quarter, we donate leftover funds to services that provide for children who come from broken homes, and last month, we bought a bus for the nursing home on Bleaker so the oldies could get out more."

I sipped my beer as pride swelled in my chest, and I remembered why Judge was voted president and why it was a fucking honor to be his second in charge. I had a lot of bad in my life, had experienced the worst of it, but Judge knew how to combat it. He knew how to weave goodness through the chaos and give everything purpose. I was a criminal, but I never felt like a criminal under his rule. I murdered for him and stole for him, but I never hurt an innocent. Sure, we liked to throw our weight around town, encourage rumors, and spook the locals, but they were safe from us. We meant them no harm, so long as they didn't get caught up in club business.

"That's really nice of you," Izzy said, glancing over her shoulder at me. Her bright eyes sparkled with adoration, her lips held in a gentle curve, a perfect soft smile. "I want to join. How do I join?"

I lifted my eyebrows. "As a patch member?"

"Not in a million fucking years," Judge answered.

She frowned, and I hated that it was so endearing. Isabelle turned to face him. "Why not?"

"Because I said so."

"I know it's not because I'm a woman. You have women in your gan—*club*."

That was true. We did have women members. Judge didn't discriminate. It didn't matter the color of your skin, your gender, or your sexual orientation. If you brought something to the table, something Judge could use, you were in with a shot. That often landed us in hot water with our brothers from other chapters who still ran a tight and exclusive ship featuring white, straight men only. In my opinion, Blondie brought plenty to the table, but only for me. Judge had no use for her, none of the men did, so the only way she could get in was through me. But it was a risk. I could lose a lot, and so could she. If I brought her in and she betrayed us—betrayed me—I'd have to hurt her. *Really* hurt her.

She looked at me again. "What do you think, Creed?"

What'd I think? I thought our MC was no place for the pretty girl in my lap. Although our chapter was progressive and inclusive, men still dominated and made sure our female members knew it. They were all sexist assholes who made sly and nasty comments. As an equal member, she'd have to deal with that—*I'd* have to deal with that—but as my woman, I could deal with it on her behalf. As my woman, none of the men would have the balls to sexualize her. I opened my mouth to tell her she had her head in the clouds, but Judge cut in.

"You're new here, Blondie, and it shows. It doesn't matter what Creed fucking thinks. I'm president, and what I say goes."

I carried on drinking my beer as she tilted her head, holding Judge in her gaze. If she wanted in, she had to fight for it. If I fought on her behalf, he'd never respect a word that flew out of her mouth.

"That's not entirely true, though, is it?" she argued. "The president of an outlaw motorcycle group can't make solo decisions. He must discuss with the other patch members in church before anything can be motioned."

I smirked as Judge thinned his eyes. "You're not gonna get patched in, Blondie. Forget it."

"Iris is a prospect. You're telling me that she's can get patched in, but I can't? She's smaller than me."

"She can shoot," I said, coming to Judge's aid. I figured I better say something before he accused me of being pussy whipped. "Best gunman I've seen."

Judge nodded in agreement, drinking more beer. When Kace brought Iris to the club, we laughed her off and she left fuming. She showed up the next day unannounced and shot a hole through Judge's beer can from yards away. She had our attention and challenged Armi to a shoot-off in the range. Iris won by one point, fair and square.

"You ever shot a gun?" I asked Isabelle, already knowing the answer, and she shook her head.

"No."

"Are you good with knives?"

She shook her head again.

"You like laying on your back?" Judge snickered, tossing an empty beer can across the firepit, and I scowled at him. "Because that's the only way girls like you ever get into the club."

It pissed me off that he saw her as a piece of meat, that sex was all she had to offer. I knew he was goading her, that he was using his own shitty technique to encourage her to tell him how bad she wanted it.

"I do like it, actually," she shot back, and I felt her body warm against mine.

She was wound tight with frustration, her voice leaving her lips in bites of attitude.

Judge grinned at her, sitting up straight. "With thirty different men? Sometimes two—maybe three—at a time?"

A subtle shudder rolled down her spine. "No…just with James."

A thick, delightful, and damn scary sensation slithered through my stomach, sinking low. I let out the breath I didn't know I was holding.

"Oh, I see." He chuckled to himself as he hunched over for a new beer. "You want old lady status."

"Old lady status?" she wondered aloud.

"Watch out for this one, Creed. She'll take half of everything you own."

"I don't understand. How old do I have to be?"

We laughed at her.

"You got on Google and read the first article you found about bikers, and the president's role, but you skimmed the rest of it?" He blew air between his lips as he cracked his can. "Old lady is just a term, but it's sacred status. Comes at a price."

"What price?"

"Judge," I warned. "Leave it."

I knew exactly where he was going with the conversation. Why? Because he was horny, probably, and he was used to me sharing my women with him. Threesomes weren't my preferred thing, but things happened. Tonight was not the night I'd share Blondie. I needed her all to myself for a while longer. I needed to be sure she could handle it before I threw her into our world.

Judge sat forward, ignoring my warning, like an asshole. "First, Creed has to deem you worthy."

"Okay." Her ocean blue eyes flickered to mine, and she peered over her slender. "Am I?"

I'd been a biker for way too long. I never thought I'd ever have to worry about having an old lady, but if I was gonna go for it, it'd be with the girl who captivated me from the beginning. If it fell to shit, at least I could say I gave it a go. *But*...I swallowed, confused. This afternoon, she was closed off to me, absorbed in her own thoughts. I gave her space since I just told her her father planned to ruin her life for his own gain. I felt she didn't believe me, didn't trust me, but now she wanted to join the MC?

To leave her world behind? Color me fucking skeptical.

"Yeah, but—"

"We have an exclusive bylaw—"

"Judge," I snapped, making Izzy jump.

He pinned me with his arrogant, amused stare, his oily irises flashing dangerously. "What?"

"Not now."

He slid his jaw together and clenched, a quirk he had whenever he thought too hard. "Jonathan's gonna want her back."

"He can't have her."

"So she's your bitch?"

Isabelle made a noise in her throat. She hated the term, even if it was one of endearment.

"Yes."

"I think she should know what she's getting into so she can make an informed decision. What do you think, Blondie?"

It was my turn to clench my jaw. He was purposely going over my head in pursuit of his own pleasure. He didn't give two shits about her comfort or whether I made her mine or not. He was bored, and he wanted his fun. Usually, I let him have it, but he couldn't have this one. Besides, it was way too soon. She'd been mine barely twenty-four hours. There was no need to bring up a situation that didn't have to take place for a long time.

"I want to know," she told him, caressing my leg. "How bad could it be?"

To a girl who'd only had two sexual partners and was tiny compared to us? Pretty damn bad. But Judge didn't care. He explained it all to her, every reason, every rule, making it clear that if she wanted to be with me, if she really wanted to be with me, I had to share her at least once.

"Oh." Isabelle cleared her throat and glanced down at her lap. "I'm not ready for that…"

Judge grinned, smug. "I guess she doesn't want you bad enough."

"Fuck off, Damon," I growled, and he laughed, sinking back into his chair.

I handed Izzy my beer and wrapped my arms around her more, holding her close to me. I kissed her hair and nuzzled into her neck. I didn't know why…maybe to comfort her. I wanted her to know I wasn't ready to share her with anyone, either. I needed to be sure before I made that kind of commitment. If I chose her, if I took her under my patch and brought her into the club as more than a girlfriend, it meant I could never have another. If she decided club life was too much and left me, I'd be destined for meaningless sex with clubwhores for the rest of my life.

As the fire died down, and we'd all had too much to drink, Judge kept baiting Iz, a pathetic attempt to lure her into a threesome. The more she drank, the more she teased back, and the more she pondered the idea of being with two men. It turned me on and made my blood boil all at once.

"What makes you think I'd choose you, anyway?" Iz asked, tipping her head on an angle.

"Baby." Judge grinned. "You'd be stupid not to. Isn't that right, Creed?"

I cut my eyes at him. "I'm starting to think Casino is a smarter choice."

"Casino is never a smarter choice." He angled himself in his chair, a stupid smug look on his face. "Maybe she likes Armi."

I bristled, and Judge laughed under his breath. It'd be a cold day in hell before I let her choose Armi. They got along well, and I hated it. Judge knew I had issues with Armi. I brought it up with him, demanded he stop asking Armi do everything for Isabelle, so it was fitting he'd use it against me.

"Maybe I like Amani," she shot back, downing the last mouthful of her fourth beer. "Maybe she does it for me."

I smirked as Judge scoffed.

"You're not fooling anyone," he said. "I listened to you come all afternoon. A pussy isn't going to do it for you."

She laughed as more heat wafted from her, and he gave me an arrogant look.

"You're right," she replied and tossed her can across the pit to the box we'd turned into a makeshift bin. She missed. "Creed is enough."

"Is he?"

As president, Judge played a verbal role. He knew what to say and when to say it, but I was always the one who put those words into action. He ran his mouth, but I got shit done. And I'd fucking prove it so he had no doubt Isabelle was mine, that I owned every inch of her perfect body. I believed it. She had me believing the whole club could line up, ready for their turn with her, and it'd still be my name she called.

I slid my hand under her over-sized sweater and cupped one of her breasts. I felt the weight of it in my hand as it spilled over the edges, and her nipple hardened.

"Yes," she said as I kissed the slope of her neck.

I knew she'd choose Judge as her provider if anything happened to me, and I wanted her to choose him, but for the moment, she was mine, and he had no right to make her skin pebble with goosebumps. Blondie relaxed into me and tilted her head, giving me more flesh to kiss. I did, gratefully, until she reached behind us and held the back of my neck, wanting more. I'd give her more. I'd give her more while Judge watched, so there was no doubt who she wanted or who she belonged to. I plunged my hand under the blanket then under the hem of her sweatpants. She sucked sharp air between her teeth as I slid my fingers along her bare pubic mound, marveling that it was still as soft and as smooth as it was last night.

I kissed Izzy more and nipped at her earlobe before I spoke in her ear.

"Show him," I whispered. "Show him I'm all you need, baby."

Izzy opened her eyes and turned her head to look at me. I expected her to shy away, but liquid courage swam in the depths of her pretty ocean pools, and she kept her eyes on me as she shifted her hips and reached under the blanket where her body heat scorched every inch of me.

"I don't have anything to prove to him," she murmured, only for me. "But I'll play your game."

She was a good girl, but I made her bad. I made her want to be bad for me. Isabelle curled her fingers around the hem of her pants and lifted her ass to push the fabric down her thighs and over her knees. I felt the burn of Judge's gaze on her from across the fire pit. I wanted to look at him and be smug, but I couldn't take my eyes off my woman. She mesmerized me with her hooded eyes and glossy lips as she glided her palm over the back of my hand and pushed it lower, guiding our fingers to the soft creases that guarded her opening. She hummed my name and slid her finger against mine, easing the both of us inside her. I groaned as she bent her knees and pushed us deeper. The blanket slipped from our legs, but neither of us made a move to grab it, and she was exposed to Judge, our hands the only thing that stopped him from seeing her most intimate part.

"That feels good," she moaned, closing her eyes and resting her head against my chest.

I squeezed her breast hard and toyed with her nipple. I pinched it hard and rolled it between my fingers, making her suck air between her teeth as she flexed her hips. Finally, I flicked my stare to Damon, who watched intently, his eyes on her breast, then her stomach, and where my finger disappeared inside her perfect pussy. He sipped at his beer and continued to watch, his excitement making his sweatpants rise. Anger and jealousy cut through my bones at the thought of him seeing her so vulnerable, but competition and pride outweighed the negative. I wanted him to covet what I had for once.

"He's looking at you," I whispered in Blondie's ear, curling my finger inside her, making her back arch. "Does that turn you on?"

She shook her head but leaked into my hand as her pussy tightened.

"Liar."

I smirked against the shell of her ear and added a second finger. She gasped and grabbed my wrist with her free hand, pushing my fingers in as deep as they would go.

"James…"

I turned my head and buried my face into her neck. I kissed, sucked, and bit her flesh until she was a quivering mess, until she was begging me to give her more, to make her come. I released her breast to rub her clit. I barely circled her little bundle of nerves three times before she went off, her orgasm taking her body my storm. I kept going until she couldn't bear my touch without giggling. Then I grabbed her and laid her flat on the daybed.

"Glad I didn't take the plastic off those cushions," Judge mused. I'd forgotten he was here. "Do I get to partake or—"

"Get lost, Damon." I kneeled between Isabelle's legs and yanked off my hoodie and shirt. "Or stay and learn how to please a woman properly. I don't give a shit."

I descended on her, and she grabbed at the hem of my pants, lifting her head off the cushions to meet my lips. Our breaths clashed as we kissed with passionate fever. My head spun, and I couldn't tell which way was up.

"Asshole," Judge muttered. Then his chair scraped the bricks below. "I'll be inside if you decide you want a real orgasm, Blondie."

This motherfucker. I broke the kiss with a tight,

angry noise in my chest, and Isabelle caught my face in her hands, bringing me back, our noses grazing. "Ignore him."

She kissed me hard and wrapped her legs around my hips, pulling me flush against her body. It was easy to ignore him when she dominated my mind, body, and soul. Seconds later, I heard the cabin's back door close and we were alone outside.

I took her on the daybed all night. I fucked her, made love to her, and kissed her until my ass, thigh, bicep, and jaw muscles ached. When it was over, when the fire turned the wood to ash, and the plastic covering the cushions was torn, we wrapped the fur blanket around us and snuggled in tight.

I just managed to doze off when the creak of a chair chased away my sleep. I opened my eyes and glanced at the dark figure sitting in Judge's seat. He struck a match, and the flame illumined Judge's tired features for a split second as he lit his cigarette. Guilt ate at me. He only smoked when he was stressed.

"Can't sleep?" I asked, my voice husky.

"Nah." He dragged on the cigarette, and the cherry glowed. "You know I can't sleep here."

I did know that. It was why we stopped coming here when Nila died. It was why I was shocked when I found out he sent Izzy here.

I cleared my throat. "Did you visit her? Did you give her the bear?"

On the way here, we stopped at a department store. I bought Izzy clothes and toiletries, and Judge bought Nila a small, pink teddy. There was a hand-carved chest attached to her headstone filled with

148

gifts he'd bought her over the years.

"Yeah."

I still remembered her funeral. No one showed except the club. We were all she had.

I glanced down at Blondie's sleeping face, at the perfect furrow in her brows. If she chose me, the club would be all she had, too. We could be the best thing that ever happened to her…

…or the absolute worst.

ELEVEN

IZZY

"Fuck!"

What the hell? My eyelids flutter open then close again. My skull thumps, my brain feeling as though it's swollen ten times its normal size. *How much beer did I drink last night?* I feel warm, naked skin against me and an erection hard against my belly. *Creed.* Memories of last night flood my mind, and a warm flush rushes through me. I snuggle closer to him, wanting to be closer, wanting to get away from the fresh morning air that nips at my skin through little openings at the edge of the blanket. Under my cheek, his skin is warm, and the thump of his heart beats at a steady pace. If I ignore the disgusting fact my father has thrown me to the wolves for his own benefit, life is perfect...

The blanket covering my body is lifted, and I squint up at the shadowy figure standing above me. "Nice ass."

Or life *was* perfect for a moment. Judge swats

me on the ass, and I shout, shielding my butt with my hand as I grab the blanket and twist on the cream daybed.

"Oh my God!" I snap, shoving myself against Creed, who grips my hip and holds me firm. "What's wrong with you?"

I blink away the fog over my eyes and glance up at the tall, broad-shouldered Damon Judge. He quirks a tidy eyebrow and lifts one side of his full lips, the beginnings of a smirk.

"Now you're shy? I practically saw your uterus last night."

"You did not," I splutter as fire rips through my cheeks, and Creed chokes on a laugh.

Judge turns his dark gaze on his VP, all sparkly traces of humor gone. "Get up. We gotta go."

My stomach drops. "Go?"

"Good-fucking-bye." Creed takes my wrist and eases my arm behind my back, pressing my palm to his hard length. "You promised me two days."

"Forget it. Ra called. The FBI is coming to the clubhouse."

Creed's body tightens, and his erection softens. "Shit."

"We gotta go to church."

Exhaling, Creed sits up, dumps more of the blanket on me, and runs his fingers through his chocolate hair. I flick my stare over his toned physique and admire the way the morning sun kisses every pore.

"Fuck," he sears, and Judge bends, grabbing Creed's clothes off the ground.

"Yep." He tosses the clothes onto the bed. "Get

dressed."

Creed curses as he grabs his hoodie and pulls it on over his head. Then he pushes the rest of the blanket off to put on his pants. While he adjusts himself, I wrap the blanket around me, doing my best to ignore Judge, who I can see out of the corner of my eye, grinning at me.

"You're covered in jizz," he points out, and I balk. "Fun night?"

"I am not!"

More heat scorches my cheeks. Has he always been so brash? Like Modo?

"Leave her alone, Damon," Creed bites out, leaving the bed. "Get dressed, Iz. We'll stop somewhere for breakfast—"

"She's not coming."

Creed cuts his eyes at Judge. "Yes, she is."

"No, she isn't. Have you forgotten why we're keeping her away in the first place?"

"I'm not staying here by myself," I protest, lifting myself off the daybed. "There could be murderers—"

"Murderers? That's your concern?" Judge laughs, flashing his perfect, white teeth. "You've been cuddling up to worse."

His words elicit a shudder from me. Creed, being as handsome, charming, and kind as he is, makes it easy to forget he lives his life on the wrong side of the law. What did he say he had to do to get here? Make someone talk? I don't want to know.

"Tell her, Creed," he adds. "She stays here."

I turn my attention to Creed and wear my best pout. Over the years, this pout has gotten me a lot of extra pocket money as a kid and out of a lot of tight spots as an adult. Creed squares his impossibly broad shoulders, straightens his spine, and purses his lips. He's the perfect picture of a VP trying to enforce his president's rule.

"That pout might work on Daddy, baby, but you've got no hope with me." He swallows, and I see the disappointment swirl in his eyes. "You're staying."

"Please, James," I say, stepping closer, craning my neck to look up at him. Beside me, Judge curses. "Something could happen to me. I don't feel safe without you."

Creed holds strong, his honey-gold eyes stern and serious. It lasts all of two seconds before he softens, like butter, and flicks his sympathetic stare to Judge.

"No, Creed. I said no. She stays."

"She doesn't want to stay by herself—"

"Oh, Jesus fucking Christ," he groans, cutting Creed off as he throws his hands and turns his back. "She's broken my VP."

* * *

I bounce down the front stairs of the cabin, barefoot, with an equal amount of fear and excitement swirling in my stomach. I drag my gaze over Creed's mechanical beast, the all-black motorcycle he apparently named Kitty. Going by the name, I didn't expect Kitty to be so…so…scary. *I'm supposed to ride on that?* Fear tips the scale in my belly. I've never been on a motorbike like

153

Creed's before. It's blacked out, every inch of it, and it looks powerful. I nervously finger the skirt of my short, floral summer dress. It's pale pink in hue and covered in a sporadic and colorful flower pattern. I didn't plan on wearing a dress for the ride, but dresses are all Creed bought.

I shift my attention from the chunky, beautiful piece of black machinery to Creed, who stands beside it. His hands are inside the pockets of his black jeans as he engages in a serious conversation with Judge, who leans against his own motorcycle. Both men are wearing their infamous leather vests—cuts. I heard Creed call it a cut—and it sends chills down my spine. Good chills. They look good.

I peer at the club's insignia that covers the expanse of Creed's wide back, and funny enough, the angry skull with the demonic horns doesn't look so scary anymore. Somehow, I've found comfort in it.

Judge's attention finds me first, and he looks at my bare legs. "A dress? I said jeans, and where are your shoes?"

"I don't have any jeans," I tell him, tiptoeing over the gravel drive. "Or shoes."

Creed turns and rakes me with his hungry gaze. My heart races, and the friction of it causes unbearable heat to rise in my throat and settle in my cheeks. No one has ever looked at me the way he looks at me, like I'm an anomaly. His esteeming stare makes me feel valued and beautiful, and for once, I feel a male's genuine appreciation in my chest. It's nice knowing Creed's longing gaze is for me and isn't a buttery ploy to get closer to my father or to syphon his contacts out of me.

"I thought you went shopping?" Judge asks Creed, scratching at his dark stubble.

"I did." Creed steps toward me, his stare glued to mine, and smiles as he extends a hand toward me. I smile back and place my hand in his. He pulls me closer to his bike. "I didn't buy her jeans."

"Why not?"

I close the distance between Creed and me, and he releases my hand to grab my waist and he lifts me into his arms. My breath hitches, and I grab onto him, my arms around his neck, as he holds me tight to him with a rough hand underneath my dress to grip my thigh. He places me on the warm leather seat of his bike, making me straddle the firm material, and flicks his thumb over my heated skin, caressing me. "I like seeing her legs."

The metal either side of my legs is warmer than warm, and the seat is thick, keeping my legs open. I hold the material of my dress down with one hand and grab Creed's large, tattooed forearm with the other, not wanting him to leave me on here by myself.

"She's not gonna have legs to look at if you tip your bike."

Creed rolls his beautiful eyes. "Have I ever tipped my bike?"

"First time for everything."

"Not today." He bends low and picks something off the ground. I eye it cautiously as he turns it upright and waves it at me, beaming wide. *A helmet?* Thank *God!* Judge snorts and throws his leg over his motorcycle then peers over his shoulder as Creed slips the black, dome helmet onto my head. "I'll go slow."

He caresses my jaw with his fingers and smiles playfully as he clicks it in and adjusts the straps.

"Do you wear a helmet?" I ask.

"Nah." He smirks, and my heart does a stupid flip. "It'll mess my hair."

I laugh then suddenly tremble at the thought of sitting like this the whole way to Exeter—which is a two-hour ride. He grins, highly amused by my uneasiness. I'm used to town cars and personal drivers, not bikers and their death-rockets. *I bet any other girl he's taken on this thing loved it.*

"You didn't bring a car?" I ask, not letting go of him, even though he's done adjusting my helmet.

"Can't access the cabin on four wheels," Judge answers. I look at him, and he snorts, smiling. "You look stupid."

I pull a face. *Stupid?* "There's nothing *stupid* about safety."

Creed hums his agreement and cranes his neck, bending over to bring his face closer to mine. "Safety is looking pretty sexy right now."

He grabs my face and kisses me between the straps of my helmet, on my jaw and my neck. His hot breath blows over my skin, and goosebumps erupt, making me laugh.

Through squinty slits, I see Judge shake his head, bewildered. "If you're done playing cute with each other," he says, "let's fucking go."

Creed beams at me then turns his back and swings his leg over the body of his motorcycle. The bike moves with him as he moves it off its stand

and kicks it back. I grab onto him, wrapping my arms around his thick torso, and hold on for dear life. I feel his body vibrate with laughter, and he reaches behind him, grabbing my thighs. With a rough tug, he pulls me hard against him and pushes my thighs into the sides of his body. The insides of my knees dig into Creed's cut, and the feel of the leather turns my hot blood to lava.

"Squeeze me with those thighs, baby."

I tighten my hold. "Like this?"

"That's better." He forces me to squeeze harder. "Hold me as tight as you do when we fuck."

Judge starts his motorcycle, and the loud rip of the engine startles me. I grip Creed out of reflex, pressing the helmet, and the side of my face, into his back.

"There you go." Creed starts his motorcycle, and the vibration from its powerful engine ripples up my legs to my core then vibrates through every limb. I squeeze my eyes shut. *Christ. Please don't let me die. I don't want to die.*

Creed lifts his foot off the ground, and the motorcycle rolls forward. He rides at a slow pace as he makes his way through the forest and the skinny, makeshift drive that quickly gives way to a tiny, dirt road. I open my eyes and peer around him at Judge, who also rides at a slower pace. *Oh. This isn't so bad.* I loosen my grip and feel Creed relax, too. Soon, the narrow dirt road gives way to asphalt, and Creed picks up speed a little at a time until my stomach feels like it's floating out of my body. *I wish I had breakfast beforehand...* I hold him tighter, and tighter, and press my head to his back

157

once more, shielding my face from the harsh whip of wind as he speeds toward the horizon, toward Exeter.

* * *

After an eternity on the road, Creed pulls into a gas station advertising hot food. Judge does, too. When Creed stops the motorcycle, weight returns to my stomach, and I sigh in relief, loosening my hold on Creed once more. The low rumble of Judge's motorcycle pounds at my left eardrum as he slowly rolls to a stop beside us.

"I'm gonna keep going," he shouts. "Unless you think you're gonna run into any trouble?"

"Not anticipating it."

Judge nods and plants his boots back onto his foot rests and rides off. A heartbeat later, the hum of Creed's engine shuts off, taking the pressure in my ears away with it. Strangely, the vibration remains between my legs, embedded in my skin.

Creed lifts himself off the bike, forcing me to let go of him. I grab onto his warm seat as he kicks down the stand and swings his leg over without kicking me with his giant boot. He straightens himself then turns toward me. I blow air from my lips and reach for the clasp under my chin, but Creed swats me away to do it himself.

"You hungry?" he asks.

I nod. "Are you?"

"I could eat."

He takes my hand in his and escorts me toward the big blue doors of the lonesome gas station. As we approach the entrance, a small handful of travelers catches my attention. Their eyes flicker between openly gawking at us and purposely avoiding eye contact. It's quiet, no one makes more noise than they should, and it's even worse once we get inside. Across the large space, conversation warbles, a register dings, and a receipt prints, then silence. A family of four turns from the counter and balks when they see Creed. The father, a plump, middle-aged man in a Hawaiian t-shirt, cautiously escorts his children around us. Their youngest, a red-headed little girl in a bright pink tutu, waves at Creed, and he kindly waves back, much to the parents' dismay. The mother pulls her daughter alongside her, shielding her with her own body as they exit the building. *Oh.* Creed is so nice to me it's easy to forget he wears a patch and has a reputation. It's easy to forget he's a symbol of anarchy, ruin, and death. I glance at Creed, who keeps his attention on the staff behind a hot-food counter, his expression indifferent. Does he even realize people are treating him like a psycho? As if they're concerned one slip and he'll murder them all? More so, what makes them fear him? The dark hair? The tattoos? The leather? Maybe it's the name sewn into the leather. The Exeter Chapter of the Devil's Cartel didn't always have a righteous Damon Judge at the helm, and I've heard the stories. I've read about the damage inflicted upon the town by the last DCMC president...before he was strung up by his neck and hung from the water tower.

I observe Creed's interaction with the public as

he orders our food, and there's a tone to his voice, a dark tone that tips toward malice. I guess he knows they fear him, and I guess he likes it that way. When he's ordered our food and has paid the shaky-handed teenage boy, he presses his palm to the small of my back and leads me outside to a square, red table. I sit in silence as he taps around on his phone. *I wish I had mine...* I haven't posted to any of my social medias in days. I haven't sent my daily Snap to Chelsea, either. Is she worried about me? Does she know I'm with Creed?

A small eternity later, Creed's name is called through quiet and crackly speakers. He retrieves the food and sets our matching breakfast dishes on the table alongside my bottle of orange juice and his strawberry milkshake. I notice, on his return, that the gas station is nearly empty.

"Is it always like this?" I ask, grabbing my small plastic fork.

He arches a brow. "Like what?"

"This." I gesture around us, at the quiet gas station. "They couldn't get into their cars fast enough. They're scared of you."

"Good." Creed laughs, delight dancing in his irises. He reaches for his milkshake and pulls out the straw, dripping pink milk on the table. Then he takes off the lid. I watch the way he deconstructs the cup to allow him to sip from the rim. "I'm a scary man."

He lifts it to his mouth and swallows a big gulp. When he lowers it, my attention falls to the bubbly, pink line of milk along his top lip, and I laugh.

"Absolutely terrifying." I pull out a small, white

160

napkin from underneath my plate and hand it to him. "For your pink milk moustache."

He graciously takes it and wipes his mouth, removing the evidence of his penchant for strawberry milkshakes from his skin and beard, and gestures for me to eat my food. The food is nothing to write home about—not-so-crispy bacon, pale eggs, and a slice of unbuttered toast. My father would destroy a food business for less…but who am I to judge? Putting my breakfast prejudices aside, I eat the food, and surprisingly, it tastes good. Real good. I lose myself to it for a moment, humming and ignoring Creed as he watches me. I don't think I've ever been so hungry.

I'm brought back to reality by a blue sedan as it flies into the gas station, rock music blasting through the cracks in the windows. It rolls to a stop beside Creed's bike, and young preppy-looking boys howl with laughter. Their laughs and good vibes flow through the parking lot and swirl around our table. It's infectious, making me smile. The ruckus draws Creed's attention, too, and when he glances over his shoulder, the guy in the passenger seat looks at the bike beside him. I watch his laugh fizzle out as he scans the station, his eyes widening when he sees Creed. I frown, and Creed turns in his seat to get a better look. The young men panic and shout before the driver puts his car in reverse and peels out the same way he came. I blink. *Wow.* Blowing annoyed air from his lips, Creed turns back to his food, placing his tattooed elbows on the table. As if it never happened, he continues to eat his breakfast. I keep my questions at bay until my curiosity is too much to bear.

"What was that about?" I ask.

"They owe me money," he simply says with a shrug. "Frat boys. Guess I'll just have to catch up with them in town."

"Money for what? Are you going to hurt them?"

He flicks his whiskey gaze from his plate to me and flashes me a playful smirk. "You expect me to answer those questions? It's club stuff, Izzy."

Club stuff. Politics operate with the same mentality. I tilt my head. "Are you carrying a gun?"

I need to know. If something happens, I need to know how things will be handled so I can mentally prepare myself. He contemplates lying to me; I can tell by the way his lids thin. Growing up in the environment I grew up in, reading expressions before words left lips was a must. *Pay attention*, my father would say. *Lips lie, but eyes don't.*

"Two," Creed finally admits then places the last bite of toast into his mouth.

"Two?" I flick my gaze over him. I held him tight on the ride here and squeezed him between my legs, but I didn't feel anything. How does he conceal them so well? More importantly, should I be concerned he felt the need to carry two weapons for our drive into Exeter? A town where the Devil's Cartel reigns supreme. "Do you plan on running into trouble?"

"I always run into trouble." He pushes his plate away, swallowing. "Hoping to avoid it since I got you with me, but I won't hold my breath."

He told Judge he wasn't anticipating any problems... Dread curls through my stomach, and sprouts of fear and regret grow. *Maybe I should've stayed at the cabin.*

At that moment, a red sedan pulls up, and an elderly couple exits the vehicle. Their gazes are on Creed's back before they've hit the button on their keys to lock the car. The elderly gentleman pauses and turns to his wife for a private discussion, and a small eternity later, she nods her head and they continue their walk toward us.

When they get within proximity of us, I make eye contact with them and smile.

"Good morning," I say, and they ignore me. In fact, they can't get out of the building fast enough.

I frown after them then look at Creed, who watches me sympathetically. It's endearing, an expression I don't think I've seen on him before.

"Am I missing something?" I ask. "Should I be more afraid of you?"

"I like that they're afraid of me. They should be." He sits back in his chair and reaches inside his cut. "But I don't want you to fear me. I don't want you to see me in that light."

Creed pulls a wild, orange flower from inside his cut, and I lift my eyebrows. It's squished and dying, but he's so proud of himself. I take the flower from his large fingers and survey it closer.

"Looked better when I picked it..." he adds. "Just didn't want to give it to you in front of Judge because, well, you know how he is."

Throughout my young life, I've received a lot of flowers—small bouquets, large bouquets, flowers wrapped in silk and lace, flowers with petals adorned with tiny diamonds that were put together by someone who didn't know me. Creed, big bad James Creed, looked at this flower and he thought of me. Then he picked it. Not bought. *Picked*. With his giant hands. I've never liked the color orange...

...but suddenly it's my favorite.

"Thank you."

My heart swells in my chest, and his small gesture puts my entire life into perspective. Aside from Chelsea, I've never had a genuine relationship in my life. They're all fake, all built on the back of my father's campaigns—even my relationship with Pierce. We only dated because our fathers insisted, and we didn't mind each other. Most of our conversations were shallow and the sex as exciting as a funeral. I was happy to settle since I didn't know any better, but one meaningful little gesture from the man most fear, the man most want to see dead, and the trajectory of my life has been changed. Who knew such a dark soul could shed so much light?

"You finished?" Creed asks, pulling me from my thoughts, pointing to my empty plate.

Rolling the stem of the beautiful, sad flower between my fingers, I nod, and he takes the plate and walks it over to the trashcan. I watch him, flicking my gaze all over him, feeling incredibly attached to this stranger.

"C'mon, Blondie," he shouts over his shoulder as he dumps our rubbish inside. "Let's go home."

TWELVE

CREED

It was the ride that transformed my life. I always rode solo, never giving up my space for anyone, especially not a piece of fender fluff, but it was different with Izzy. It felt right to have her thighs around me, her head against my back. I drove carefully, never breaching the speed limit, slowing at every corner or when she gripped me tighter. I wanted her to enjoy it. I wanted her to want to ride with me again and again. She'd never know it, but it was intimate for me to have her on the back of my bike, as intimate as kissing. She was the first to sit there, the first to hold me while I rode. I swore I'd never do it and made fun of any member that did, but we all had exceptions, and Blondie was mine. I knew it the moment I laid eyes on her.

And it was totally fucking crazy to think the way I was after such little time together. She could be a complete fucking wackjob for all I knew...

...she could also be the love of my life.

Didn't know which was scarier. I huffed to myself, embarrassment trickling through my veins at the thought of anyone hearing what was going through my mind. I fucking hated clichés, but I learned a long time ago that life was one cliché after another. I was a cliché, she was a cliché, and together, we made a giant clichéd mess.

As we crossed the town's limits, hair prickled on the back of my neck. We flew past the welcome sign, and I caught a flash of sun reflecting off metal. I peered into my right mirror and watched as police cars pulled out of the shrubbery and onto the asphalt. Sirens squealed, the high ring making me wince, and Isabelle squeezed me.

"James!" she shouted, her fingers twitching against my stomach. "Are we in trouble?"

I glanced at my mirrors again as the single line of vehicles split in two, a cop car flanking each side. I ran a few scenarios in my head. I couldn't outrun them, not on this bike, not with Blondie on the back. I was left with no choice. I indicated and left the road, pulling onto the shoulder. The sirens stopped, but the lights remained on. I released my drag bars and sat back, easing myself against Isabelle. Then I turned my head until I could just see her face out of my peripheral. She was wide-eyed and frightened under her helmet, under my favorite black brain bucket.

"It's all right," I told her. "Was going a little over the limit and I'm not wearing a helmet. We're okay."

Iz relaxed her grip, but I sat taller, straightening my spine and squaring my shoulders. I lied to her.

The cops were waiting for us. We were exactly where they wanted us to be, and that put me on edge. Did they stop Judge, too? Or was Blondie the one they want? I looked into my side mirrors and watched as car doors opened. One officer appeared, then two. In a matter of seconds, six cops were walking toward us, cautiously fingering the black handguns still holstered to their hips. I clenched my jaw. *What the fuck am I going to do?*

"There's so many of them…" Isabelle said, still holding me tight. "This isn't because you were speeding at all, is it?"

I shook my head.

"Turn off your motorcycle," a baritone voice demanded. "*Now.*"

I slowly moved my hand toward the key and turned off my bike. Then the sounds of gravel crunching underneath shoes drew closer, accompanied by a crackly warble from their radios.

"James Creed," the same, deep voice shouted. "You're under arrest for—"

"What?" Isabelle shrieked, and the motorcycle shook as she whipped her head in their direction.

I blew frustrated air out of my lips, kicked my bike stand down, and turned. "Under arrest?"

"Don't fucking move!" they ordered, but I lifted myself off the bike anyway.

Izzy gasped and dropped her hold to grip the seat instead. The six officers stopped, their guns drawn, their beady scowls focused on Blondie and me. I reached inside my cut and around to my lower back and pulled my revolver from my waistband. The officers drew their own weapons, and I was staring down the barrels of more guns than I'd like.

"Haven't hurt a hair on her head," I said, my fingers twitching around the handle of my gun. "Jonathan—"

I swallowed my words as half the officers turned their guns on Isabelle. A pang of panic slammed into my gut, and for the first time in a long time, I didn't know what to do.

"It's not your town anymore," the cop in front said, and I focused on him, on his buzz cut, his black uniform that clung tight to his overweight body, and the shiny badge on his chest. "Drop your weapon, get on your knees, and put your hands behind your head."

"Or what?" I stepped forward. "You'll shoot me?"

"James…" Isabelle whispered, her voice trembling.

I ignored her. If they wanted to shoot me, they would've already. There was an ulterior motive at play here, and I wasn't going to go down quietly.

"No. I won't shoot you." The corners of his lips quirked. "You can come with us now, or we'll pick you up later. Doesn't bother me."

So, they wanted Blondie? I lifted my arm and pointed my Smith and Wesson at Isabelle, the barrel of it pointed perfectly in the space between her eyebrows. The pigs tensed and shuffled nervously, their eyes wide with worry. Isabelle choked, and I did my best to block the terrified noises she made from my head. I had to get us out of here by any means necessary. If I had to shoot her, I would. *I think.*

"You want her?" I asked, pulling back the hammer until my gun clicked.

My stomach churned at the thought of what I was doing, at the thought of any harm coming to her by my hands or the hands of these fuckers.

The cop at the front, the overweight one with the buzz cut, sneered at me. "Go ahead. Shoot her. The more battered she is, the better."

I clenched my jaw. They really were gonna use her to bring us down, huh? That had to be the weakest game plan ever. She'd never lie and say I hurt her. She'd never testify against me or Judge or the Devil's Cartel. I stole a glance at her, and she pleaded silently with kinks in her brow and a trembling lower lip. Would she? *Bang!* Isabelle's face twisted in pain, and she howled, clenching her bicep. *What the fuck?* I lowered my gun, shocked, as blood trickled over her slender fingers. I whipped my head back to the police.

"Shots fired! Requesting back up," the lardy pig squealed into his radio. *Bang!* Another shot rang out, and Isabelle shrieked. I snapped my attention to her, to the bullet hole in my goddamn seat right by her bare thigh. "Drop your weapon or my next bullet goes in her spine."

Without thought, I lifted my gun and shot him. In my rage, I missed my mark, and the bullet tore through the side of his neck. He crashed to the ground, shouting, gurgling, and clenching his bleeding neck. As he squirmed, all guns turned to Izzy, and I was caught in a checkmate. They knew I wasn't going to hurt her, and I knew they *would* hurt her. They fucking had me. Izzy whimpered, and her eyes glistened, silently pleading for me to end this standoff. *Jesus Christ.*

"All right!" I shouted, tossing my gun away.

A thick, heavy feeling wormed its way through my stomach, and I felt sick. I hated myself. I never fucking threw in the towel, but here I was, throwing my gun to the ground and getting on my knees, uncaring that hard pieces of gravel dug into my kneecaps through my jeans. Isabelle mumbled her apologies through tears, and I was yanked by my collar and forced onto my stomach before I could acknowledge her. I *just* managed to turn my head as the side of my face hit the gravel.

"Easy!" I snapped, creating little whirlwinds of dust with my breath.

Whoever was on me responded by digging their hard knee between my shoulder blades and burying their hard elbow into my neck. I hissed, and they pushed harder. Through the pain, I watched a lady pig pull Izzy off my motorcycle and roughly cuff her. Blood ran freely down Blondie's arm, turning her pale complexion red and ruining the pretty dress I chose, the one that cost me a small fortune. In the next heartbeat, my arms were wrenched behind me and I was cuffed and lifted to my feet, a cop flanking each side of me. Up ahead, the man I shot was being tended to, and in the distance, the sirens of their approaching backup sang. He'd be okay. I only grazed him, like he grazed Izzy.

"You'll be all right," I teased as they marched me past him. "It's only a scratch, pussy."

I was shoved forward by a forceful heel of a palm to the middle of my back, and I snickered.

170

This was a giant waste of my time. By this evening, I'd be a free man, and every single one of these assholes, these *puppets*, would pay with their blood.

Twenty yards out from the police cruisers, Izzy was veered off to the left and me the right. As we approached the back of the cruiser, the door opened, and out stepped the last man I thought I'd see. *Jonathan Laurent.* I felt my face warp into a scowl so tight my eyebrows ached. I took him in in his dark gray suit and his blue and white tie, and the fucker had the audacity to smirk at me. He sat back here and let them shoot at Isabelle? What the fuck was wrong with him? I shrugged out of the grasp of those holding me and charged forward.

"You fuckin—" I was hit from behind, tackled to the ground, and my face kissed the gravel once more.

"James!" Isabelle shouted, then her voice was muffled by glass as the back door to the police cruiser carrying her was shut.

The asshole on my left buried his fingers in my hair and yanked my head up. He wretched me back onto my knees, and I grunted as Jonathan grinned down at me.

"Not so tough without your gang," he sneered, the blue and red lights from the roof of the car coloring his silvery hair.

"Don't need 'em," I said, breathless. "Uncuff me and I'll show you."

His wicked eyes flashed at the challenge, but I knew he wasn't pondering the idea. Jonathan was many things, but he wasn't a fighter. He preferred to fight a mental battle, a battle of wits, of cunning.

If he needed something physically sorted, he called his pigs to do it.

"You're going away for a long time." He glanced toward Izzy's car. "Your whole club is."

"Oh, yeah?" I laughed. "You're delusional."

The skin around Jonathan's eyes crinkled as he faked a smile. "Am I?"

"You think she'll lie for you? You think she'll betray me?" I shook my head and laughed again. "She's mine. I made her mine. She has no loyalty to you, the man who threw her to the wolves." I shuffled closer on my knees. "The wolves have been good to her. *Too* good."

Jonathan's jaw tightened and relaxed as he clasped his hands in front of him, down low. "My daughter's loyalty lies wherever I want it to. She's easily bought, easily persuaded. It's not her fault; she gets it from her mother." He leaned forward, bringing his face level with mine. "She knew all along what I needed in order to disassemble the Devil's Cartel. Of course, I'd prefer Damon Judge kneeling in front of me, but she insisted you'd be the easier one to manipulate, and she was right." Delight glistened in his irises as doubt sprouted in my chest. *Did she fucking play me?* "You didn't think your time with her was real, did you?"

I pursed my lips and looked over to Isabelle, who pressed herself to the glass window of the cruiser, mortification plain on her face. I did find it odd she wasn't concerned with her father whereabouts or whether he was dead or alive, but who would? He was a damn snake.

I'd experienced plenty of fake relationships, and

fake interactions, throughout my life. There was nothing phony about Isabelle Laurent or the time we spent together.

And I'd bet my patch on it.

THIRTEEN

IZZY

My chest heaves. I'm alone. Trapped in a sparse, beige room with nothing but a steel table and a plastic stool. I glance up from the gray, speckled table surface to the mirrors in front of me. I've seen enough *Law and Order* shows to know they're two-way. Regardless of who may be watching, I stare at myself in the reflection. This morning, I was clean and cute. Now...now I look like a homeless criminal. My long, blonde hair is a tangled mess, my eyes puffy from crying, and there are dried drops of blood all over me. At least they patched the bullet graze on my arm when I got here—here being Exeter's only police station. Where's Creed? Is he here, too? Does Judge know?

A clang in the door draws my gaze, and I tighten as it swings open, revealing a face I never want to see again. Dad saunters across the threshold, proud of himself, with a badge-wearing thug in tow.

"Belle, sweetheart," Dad greets me, crossing the

small room to cup my face in his large hands. He swipes his thumbs down my cheeks and collects my tears. "I'm glad you're okay."

He perches on the edge of the table, and the door clangs again, locking me inside with this…this…*stranger.* I lift my gaze to meet his, and my blood cools in my veins, then I pull my face out of his hold and shove my chair back, creating distance between us. Dad threads his fingers and rests his hands on his lap. Exhaling, he tilts his head and pins me with his blue stare.

"I know you're upset—"

"Upset?" I shout, my voice cracking. "Upset doesn't begin to cover it. How could you?"

For a flicker of a moment, sympathy flashes over Dad's features only to be swallowed up by his resolution. He doesn't care about me. Not at all.

"Do you remember the story we read together during your freshman year? *Faithful Elephants*?"

I cut my eyes at him, my gut turning as I recall the story. It's a true tale about elephants in a zoo in Tokyo during World War ll. The zookeepers were ordered to poison their large and dangerous animals to prevent harm to the general public if a bomb were to detonate near the zoo and the animals escaped. It's a tale about murder for the greater good.

"Don't you dare tell me what you've done is for the greater good."

"I made a promise—"

I shoot out of my chair, and the back of my thighs hit the plastic, and the chair falls over, slapping against the concrete floor. "I am your daughter! Not a pawn, not a cog, not bait—"

"I know." Dad lifts himself off the table.

I tighten my shoulders as he approaches with caution then surrounds me with his arms, pulling me close to his chest. I inhale. He smells different, and his hug isn't bringing me the same comfort it did as a child.

"I'm sorry." He kisses the top of my head and holds me tight. "You can fix this, Isabelle. You can help me make it better, help me keep my promise so we can go back to normal—"

Fix it? I shove him, the heels of my palms hitting him hard in the chest, forcing air from his lungs. He stumbles back, his eyes wide. I've never felt anger so potent, so thick, in my veins.

"I'm not going to help you. This is *your* mess. Fix it on your own."

Dad's expression shifts, and shadows pool under his eyes and in the hollows of his cheeks as he lowers his chin. "You'll make a statement—*live.*"

"A statement?" I scoff, crossing my arms over my chest. "About what?"

He takes a calculated step forward, sending chills down my spine. "You'll tell the town, the whole United States, what you suffered at the hands of those men."

I frown. What is he talking about? "You were there when the police pulled us over. Did I look like I was suffering?"

He took another step, clenching his hands at his sides. "They kidnapped you, Belle. They hurt you, *raped* you—"

I balk. "What? No, they didn't."

The officer by the door shuffles around the edge of the room, moving closer to where I stand opposite my dad. His dark features are zeroed in on me, his bushy brows furrowed, his lips pursed into a thin line. Hairs lifts on the back of my neck. Is he going to hurt me? I look at my father. His expression is much the same. Agitated.

"They hurt you, Isabelle," Dad insists, resolute. "Real bad."

I square my shoulders and lift my chin. "Do I look hurt?"

It hits my face without warning, a fist so hard my jaw is thrusted from its natural position and cracks in my ears. I hit the floor, only just managing to get my hands out in time to catch myself. Pain radiates through my wrists, my face, and down my spine, and I taste blood. It's metallic and gross on my tongue. I lift my head and peer at the man towering over me, the one Dad brought into the room with him. He clenches his large fist at his side, his knuckles pink. Tears of surprise and pain pool in my eyes.

"What are you doing?" I cry, feeling the right side of my face throb and swell.

"They hurt you," Dad repeats, and I shake my head, turning my body. "*He* hurt you."

He? "James didn't hurt me. He kept me safe. The Devil's Cartel—"

Dad's thug bends and bunches my dress at the collar, I lift my hands to shield my face, and he swats them away with a growl then backhands me in the mouth. I shout as my lip splits against my teeth, and more blood saturates my tongue. I squeeze my eyes shut. The pain that explodes from the impact is sharp and brief, morphing into numbness.

"He hurt you. *Raped* you."

Why does he keep saying that? I spit blood on the floor and open my eyes. I can't see Dad through the blur of my tears, but I keep my stare firmly locked on his fuzzy shape regardless.

"Rape? I *begged* him to take whatever he wanted from me, and he did, multiple times, and I *loved* it. Does that sound like rape to you?"

He sucks a sharp breath between his teeth. I've hurt him with my confession, but it's true. Creed didn't have to persuade me to sleep with him or force it. I've been ready and willing from the moment I laid eyes on Creed. Dad must know that. He listened to all my therapy sessions, after all.

Dad nods, a slight movement I barely catch, and I'm hit in the face again. The sound is sickening as something in my nose pops and hot liquid gushes down my face. My head spins, and I try to lift my hands to protect myself, but they don't budge. Soon, the thug's violent hands are swapped for brutal kicks, and each boot to my body sends unbearable pain through me. I weakly clench my body as best I can as my ribs are cracked, my organs pummeled, until agony-laced darkness envelops me.

I'm not sure how much time passes before my lids flutter and I catch a blurred glimpse of expensive, black shoes by my face and the hemline of Dad's luxurious pants. I try to speak, try to tell him to get away from me, but only a whimper falls out. I'm badly hurt, my body silently screaming with every breath I take.

The loud clank from the door clangs around the room, then there's a crack from Dad's knees as he bends low and brushes hair from my cheek. I wince at the acute tenderness of my face and the gross feel of my hair sticking to drying blood.

"It's for the good of the town," he whispers. "I'll make it up to you, I promise."

I shiver, closing my eyes. "I hate you."

"You don't hate me."

"I do. I hate you. Creed will murder you for what you've done."

"You really think he cares? He'll be onto a new clubwhore as soon as he's out of prison." Dad smirks. "That's *if* he gets out after the story you're going to tell."

"I'm not doing anything for you."

"You will." He flicks my forehead, and I open my eyes. He holds his phone screen in front of my face, but I can't make out the video playing. "You see that?"

I blink, long and slow, until my eyes focus. It's a woman tied to a chair. Her head hangs forward, her long, brunette hair dangling in front of her and her beige pants dirtied and spattered with blood. Shadows move around the poorly lit room, and for a moment, a tattooed forearm is all I see. Sighing, my eyelids fall shut, and I doze off, only to be flicked on the nose. I yelp, my eyes shooting open.

"Watch," Dad demands. "Then you can sleep."

The man, with the snake forearm tattoo, saunters toward the woman in the chair whose shoulders shake like mine. I glance at his leather cut, at the blurry insignia on the back that I don't recognize. The man grabs the woman by the hair, and she shrieks as he forces her head back.

"Please," she sobs, and my skin prickles as ice slides through my veins. "No more."

I continue to watch the video and the violent events that unfold. It takes me forty-three seconds to realize who the woman in the chair is. *Chelsea.* A choked noise leaves my throat, and Dad turns off the screen, lowering his hand.

"You'll make the statement, sit through all the court proceedings, and do exactly as you're told, or Chelsea dies."

Dies? I'm going to puke. How did this get so out of control? When did my father become a murderer? I close my eyes as my body violently trembles. My thoughts scatter, and I'm powerless to organize them again. I close my eyes as tiredness zaps me and my consciousness is siphoned. I feel like my bones are crumbling. I don't want to lie and betray Creed, Judge, or the Devil's Cartel crew…

…but what choice do I have?

FOURTEEN

CREED

Two days.

Two days had passed since Izzy and I were pulled over by those pig-fuckers under her father's instruction. I grew angrier with every second I was stuck in this tiny cell. They wouldn't give me my phone call. I hadn't contacted anyone, not Judge or our lawyer, but that didn't surprise me since the building I was being held in wasn't the police station or the courthouse. I'd been in those buildings more times than I could count, and they were nicer than this shithole.

Not for the first time, my mind drifted to Blondie. Was she safe? Was she worried about me? Was her father filling her head with more lies or, worse, physically hurting her? I drummed my fingers against the metal edges of my mesh cot and exhaled. Outside the entrance to my cell, a small television sat on a stand with wheels. It'd been there for hours, rolled in by a short guy with bright red hair. I asked him a few questions, and he ignored me, the dick. I exhaled again, more dramatic this time. I could go with a goddamn cigarette…

A few heartbeats passed before the sound of shoes tapping along the concrete floor echoed through the building. Then in entered the redhead. I sat forward, resting my elbows on my knees, and watched as he stalked toward the TV and turned it on. What I was about to see had something to do with the club or Blondie. I didn't give a shit about anything else.

I held my breath as he flicked through the stations, stopping on our local news channel. The backdrop was a hospital, further wrenching my stomach, and the man the camera was steadily focused on was Jonathan. My ears twitched, and I lifted myself off the cot, the metal bars squeaking under my weight. I sauntered closer, and Red's eyes were on me, smug as he surveyed me.

"It's a battle we've fought for a long time, and at cost to my family, it'll finally come to an end," Jonathan said as he swallowed hard and avoided looking into the camera. "I didn't want to do it this way, but my daughter nobly insisted she address the public about the horrors she's suffered at the hands of the Devil's Cartel in hopes to ignite change and encourage the government to better aid us in our fight to clean the streets once and for all."

What the fuck? I grabbed the cold cell bars as movement in the background drew my attention. I flicked my stare over the shoulders of a man wearing an expensive navy suit. He was slightly hunched forward, pushing something. Jonathan's entourage moved out of the way, giving the man space to move through. I saw her then...and my heart fell into my boots. Most of Isabelle's small, battered body was hidden behind a blue hospital gown that looked more like a queen-sized bedsheet on her. For the limbs that did show, they were more purple than pale. *What the fuck did he do?* Izzy hid her face, her long, blood-stained blonde hair working as curtain between her and me, and concerned whispers floated from the small speakers. Jonathan kneeled beside her, touching her hair, playing the role of concerned father when he was the reason she was in this mess in the first place. The more he touched her, the more defeated she looked. He brushed her hair away from her face, and my breathing stopped. I swore. Her pretty face was beaten and bruised, her eyes almost swollen shut, her nose hidden behind gauze and tape. There was a huge lump on her cheek, and I could see the cracks in her lips from here.

"Jesus," Red said on exhale, moving in front of the TV, blocking my view. "He did a number on her, didn't he?" I clenched the bars harder. "Serves her right."

Red straightened his black tee and went back to leaning against the stand, his arm draped over the top of the TV. There was an amused glint in his eye, one that begged me to take the bait, but I couldn't drag my stare from Isabelle. What this fucker said to me wasn't a priority. I'd disembowel him once I got out of here; that was a fact.

Jonathan lovingly cupped Isabelle under the chin and made her look at him. She trembled and tried to pull her face away, but he moved to whisper in her ear. Her swollen and terrified gaze flickered to the camera, and my heart smashed into my ribs, filling my veins with...with...her pain. I was helpless—*useless*. I couldn't help her. When Jonathan was done whispering to her, he stood and detached the microphone from the stand and lowered it to Isabelle's mouth. He patted her hair and gently touched her arms. Izzy opened her mouth, and all that came out was a cracked sob. Her bruised face crinkled in pain, and she hunched her body and clenched her ribs.

"Perhaps she needs time, Mr. Mayor," a woman in the sea of reporters who stood behind the camera shouted.

"She's fine," Jonathan insisted. "She wants to do it now."

He nudged her, and she breathed heavy into the microphone.

"I've suffered for days," she wheezed, her voice sounding nothing like her. "I was beaten..."

I frowned, feeling my face screw up. She wouldn't lie to appease her father, would she? She had to know we were stronger than him. My blood ran cold. Did she know what would happen to her if she spoke our names on television? The men would call for her head, and there'd be nothing I could do about it. The Devil's Cartel had a chapter in nearly every state. They'd come for her, and they'd make her pay. They'd make this whole fucking town pay.

I waited with bated breath as Izzy took her time to recover between every word she spoke. I silently willed her not to say it, not to lie and put a target on her back, when banging sounded off in the distance, growing closer and closer. Red noticed it too and turned toward the door.

"What the hell is that?" he wondered aloud, pulling his handgun from the waistband of his black cargo pants.

The door to the sector I was held in swung open with enough force to drive the door into the concrete opposite, and I saw the manbun first then the rifle. Light exploded from the end of Armi's rifle, and a juddering bang rang out, leaving a ring in my ears. Red crashed to the floor, and the fucking TV blew up, sending me back a few steps as glass cut at my face and neck.

Judge barreled in behind Armi and tugged on the black skull bandana covering his mouth. I took them in in their colors, proud as fucking punch to call them my brothers. Didn't expect them to come looking for me, not in the middle of an FBI sting or while I was in custody, but here they were, raising hell.

Armi moved toward Red and bent low, patting him down. While he did that, I scowled at Judge, and he grinned. "Thought we forgot about you, did ya?"

"Two fucking days, Judge."

He shrugged his shoulders, stuffing his handgun into his cut then into the waistband of his black jeans. "Quit your bitching. We had the FBI to deal with."

I straightened. "They didn't find anything?"

Judge smirked. "Didn't find nothing. We're good."

Good. We kept the clubhouse clean, mostly, but sometimes things got delayed and left for longer than they should.

"Shit," Armi shouted, standing up. He turned and flashed us a police badge before he dropped it onto Red's lifeless body. "He's a cop."

Judge shrugged. "Not the first cop I've shot in the last forty-eight hours."

I arched a brow. "Aren't they all cops?"

Armi shook his head and dangled a set of keys between his fingers. "Twisted Sons mostly."

I grunted. I hated that they were on our territory, on *our* side of the country. "I wonder how much Jonathan is paying them and what they're getting out of it."

As Armi approached my cell, his boots crushed glass and left bloody imprints on the concrete floor. He unlocked my cell, and I stepped out.

He smiled and clapped me on the shoulder. "Good to see you, VP."

"Yeah." I shrugged him off and headed toward the door.

I had to get to the hospital. Izzy needed my help. When I was done helping her, I'd pull her father's spine out through his stomach.

Armi and Judge followed without a word, and in the halls, the carnage they left was sprayed up the walls. I stepped over every dead body as they came. I'd seen grosser, more twisted things in my time. Blood was as traumatizing as water to me.

Outside, I was surprised to see an empty parking lot in the middle of nowhere. I turned to look at the building. It was tall and made of gray stone. It had turrets either side of the roof and bars on its windows. It reminded me of my time in the detention center when I was a teen.

"What the hell is this place?" I asked Judge.

Was I even still in Exeter? I lived here most of my life and had never seen this building before.

"It's a home for troubled youth." Judge shrugged his large shoulders. "Or it was meant to be."

"Jonathan and the council had it built a long time ago," Armi chimed in.

"What happened?"

"Investors dropped out, and he couldn't keep it running on his own funds, so he canned it." He spat on the floor and scratched at his forehead. "Heard they were gonna bulldoze it and turn it into a youth camp site."

I paused then, as we walked further onto the parking lot. "Where's my bike?"

Judge laughed and shot me a look over his shoulder. "You're riding on the back of mine."

Over my dead body. I stopped in my tracks and turned around. Armi laughed as I headed back toward the entrance of the building.

"Where're you going?"

I flipped him off. "Rather rot in prison than be seen on the back of your bike, Damon."

I wasn't fender fluff. Not in a million years. If Judge rocked up at the clubhouse with me on the back of his bike, I'd never live it down. I could see the twisted faces of the men now, hear their cackling. I wasn't giving Modo more material to use against me. Besides, I didn't have the anatomy to be fender fluff.

Judge howled with laughter. "I'm kidding. We brought Armi's cage."

I stopped and turned, and Judge pointed to the shrubbery on the far side of the lot. I headed in that direction, passing Armi on the way. I pushed through the shrubs, and as we reached the cage, I grabbed the passenger side door and yanked it open. "Shotgun."

"Oh, get fucked," Armi growled. "It's my truck."

"I'm not sitting in the back." I climbed in and made myself comfortable. "I out rank and out man you."

He snorted, moving to the back door. "How do you *out man* me?"

"Don't wear my hair in a bun like a ballerina for starters."

Judge snickered as he climbed into the driver's side and slammed the door.

"Last time I save your ass, Creed," he grumbled. "You can break yourself out of prison next time."

* * *

At the clubhouse, it felt good to be home, but the feeling was fleeting. The men avoided my gaze as I walked through the door behind Judge. My stomach twisted, like cloth in a ringer. I knew it had something to do with Izzy. She was gonna give a live statement about the things we allegedly did to her. Did she follow through?

"What'd she say?" I demanded, stalking toward the main table where most of our main men—and woman—sat, dread painted across their features.

"What the fuck did she say?"

I barked at them out of fear. I feared what I was about to hear and what was to come if she lied. I feared for her safety, and I feared for myself because I cared for her. I knew I'd do something stupid to protect her from harm—even from my brothers.

Casino cleared his throat, sat back in his chair, and ran his fingers through his short hair. "She threw her father under the bus."

My frown faded, and my eyebrows lifted of their own accord. *Thank-fucking-God.* I straightened my spine and licked my lips.

"What's with the faces then?" Judge demanded, crossing the floor to the head of the table. "Who died?"

I held my breath. Behind me, Armi toyed with his rifle. An annoying habit he had whenever he held one. I closed my fists at my sides as the silence from my men planted seeds of rage in my blood. The seeds grew into saplings as images of Isabelle filtered through my mind. She was a trust fund baby raised with a silver spoon in her mouth. There wasn't a sliver of hard muscle on her body. She didn't stand a chance against her father, or anyone, really. I was all she had to keep her safe. *We* were all she had.

"They pulled her away while she screamed for you." Casino avoided my gaze as he spoke, focusing on a spot on the table instead. "Jonathan claimed she was sick. He spun his own twisted tale about the things we did to her. She was in bad shape, VP. Did Jonathan do that? To his own daughter?"

"You sound surprised," Ayr muttered. "He's fucking vile."

I turned from the table and headed back toward the front door. I didn't care what Jonathan said or the lies he told the world. We'd deal with him. I needed to get to Isabelle, and I needed to get her somewhere safe. When she was safe, I'd burn the rest of the town to the ground and we'd fuck in the ashes of my destruction.

"Where're you going?" Judge called to me—and not for the first time today.

It pissed me off that he felt he had to ask. He was president, sure, but he didn't fucking own me. "To the hospital."

"She's not at the hospital," Casino said. "Rah already looked."

Before I turned to ask where she was, Kace sauntered into the room. He wore his usual brown cut and carried a medium-sized box in his hands.

"Hey," he greeted, and I noticed he was paler than usual, his gaze spaced, his face gaunt.

"Please tell me there's cake in that box," Modo called out, jingling his keys. For as long as I knew him, he carried a small fork on his keychain he used only for surprise cake. "I could go with some cake."

"Um," Kace murmured and extended the box to me. "There's a head in here."

I stared at him, at the box he held in his hands, and dread crept over me like an icy chill, numbing me all over. Only one thought floated through my head. *Blondie's head is in the box.* Swallowing hard, I peered over my shoulder at Judge, who stood still, his shoulders squared.

"If you don't take it, I'm gonna puke on it."

I looked back to Kace and took the box, relieving the poor kid. The second the box left his hands, he whirled around and hunched over, gripping his knees. I turned and walked the box to the table. Then, without pause, I tipped the box and dumped its contents onto the table.

Most jolted backward in their seats as a head hit the wooden surface with a squelch and rolled until her lifeless eyes stared up at the high ceiling.

"What the fuck?" Modo shouted. "That's not cake."

The first thing I noticed was the blood-stained brunette hair. It was messed up, but I released a sigh of relief. It wasn't Isabelle. Somewhere, there was a gag then the sound of puking.

"Chelsea," Armi said, placing his rifle on the table. "That's Chelsea."

Izzy's friend? The clubwhore? I lifted my stare to Judge, who clenched his jaw. We'd received heads before, so this wasn't anything new. We'd handle it like we always did.

With motorcycles, guns, rage, and fire. When we're done, there'd be nothing left of Jonathan Laurent—not a legacy, not even a whisper.

"Find Jonathan." Judge turned his glare on Casino. "I want him dead by nightfall."

FIFTEEN

IZZY

I come to with a groan. There's an ache in every bone, muscle, and hair follicle in my body, growing worse with every thump of my heart. I don't know what happened after I shouted my father's crimes into the camera. I was hauled away on my wheelchair and injected in my thigh by something that put me to sleep in seconds.

I groan again and blink, trying to focus on something, trying to find a sliver of light, but the darkness is absolute. I realize, then, that the air isn't moving. Where the hell am I? I lift my arms, and my forearms hit a wooden panel. I gasp, and my breathing picks up. I taste metal and varnish on the back of my tongue, and suddenly, the darkness feels like it's closing in on me, squeezing me tightly. Out of reflex, I lift my leg and my toes hit the wood above me. I scream and thrash and scratch. Panic overrides my pain, and I don't stop until my fingernails are lifted and broken, until I'm too exhausted to move. I pant, my chest rising and falling quickly, sucking up my small allowance of air.

"Help!" I shout until my lungs burn and my voice gives out.

My voice seems to carry further than the box's limits, and I take solace in the fact I'm not buried six feet underground. I swallow hard and lift my hands again. I run my palms along the smooth wood and search for something—*anything*—but my fingers don't find a lock or a seal, not even a crack. *I can't breathe.* I gulp air and pull my limbs as close to myself as I can, trying to make my space bigger. *Oh my God. I'm going to die. I'm going to run out of air and die painfully.*

"Please!" I call out, and there's a metal screech, the sound of an overused door or an unoiled lever. I strain my ears. "Hello?"

I speak, but my voice is all wrong. It doesn't sound like me. I sound broken, like I've been smoking for eighty years or like someone has a tight grip on my throat. Warmth pools in at the soles of my feet. At first, I think I imagine it, but it grows hotter, and I realize it's not a symptom of my panic. It's something outside. As my eyes adjust, I focus on the tiniest glimmer of light at the base of my long box. It's orange and moving—no, *flickering*. Heat wafts through the box, burning up my body to engulf my chest, my neck, and my face. I whimper and struggle against my confines as sweat bubbles all over me. I jolt as my prison moves, and the sounds of a machine whir underneath me. Cogs click and whoosh, and the heat by my feet becomes unbearable. Excruciating. Unlike anything I've ever felt. The pain isn't sharp, like a needle or a knife, nor is it aching like a bruise. It's how I imagine the sun to feel, or worse. I try to pull my legs away, but my knees hit the barrier. I scream and thrash so hard I feel my wrist snap and taste blood in my mouth, in my throat. I don't care. I keep going until I can't.

Until my feet begin to blister.

Until it feels as though my soul is being drawn from my body by the heat, promising relief from the pain. In the distance, there's a bang, multiple bangs, and the sound of gunfire. At least, I think it's gunfire. I let my head loll to the side. *Maybe it's rain...or the distant sound of thunder.* The noise brings Creed to the forefront of my mind, and my heart aches. *He's a lot like thunder...*

Whatever the sound is, I welcome it.

SIXTEEN

CREED

It'd come down to this. Jonathan Laurent, the mayor of this town, was a dead man. So were all that followed his instruction. There'd be no mercy, no captives, no fucking bargaining, and we'd take the fallout as it came. Judge agreed. Blondie was mine, and after tonight, everyone in this town would know it.

We showed up on our motorcycles, in full colors, our insignia displayed proudly on our cuts, and exploded through the crematorium, without fear, throwing stealth to the wind. Before their deaths, these assholes would learn the Devil's Cartel MC hit their enemies like a freight train and left no survivors. They'd learn we didn't hide behind hidden agendas, laws, or political arguments, that we weren't afraid of repercussions or death, and we protected what was ours from anyone who threatened it. Like an avalanche, we were an unstoppable force that left nothing but rubble in our wake.

I stormed through the building without thought to what was waiting around any corner I passed by. I killed cops, bikers, anyone who stood in my way, and I did it without hesitation. Sweat bubbled along my skin and not from the fight I'd put up since arriving. It was damn hot in here, and I prayed to a God I didn't believe in that I wasn't too late. If I was…

If I was…I didn't even want to think about it.

I stepped around a corner, and the butt of a shotgun slammed into my face. Blood gushed over my tongue and out of my nose. Grunting, I stumbled backward, cupping my face, only to be caught by the back of my cut. *What the fuck?*

"Fuck, Creed!" Judge boomed as he yanked me out of the way.

Bang! I winced as my left eardrum exploded, and a ringing sound pierced my brain. The guy with the shotgun hit the floor like a sack of potatoes. Judge shouted in my ear, and I shrugged out of his grip.

"Pay more attention," he snapped, his nostril flaring. "I'd rather a dead Blondie over a dead VP."

I wouldn't.

"You seen Jonathan?" I asked, rolling my shoulders to get my cut on right.

"No." He swiped at his forehead. "Is it fucking hot in here?"

In my stomach, dread piled on top of more dread. I nodded, wiped blood from my face, and marched forward, stepping over the dead body. Ahead, two big doors stood tall, and there was a glow around the edges of the round windows in the center. Was

Izzy in there? I barreled forward and kicked the doors open. The room was hot, and the air was thick, feeling heavy in my lungs.

I saw it then…the casket on the conveyor belt and the flames that flickered at the foot of it, heating the big chamber.

Then I heard it…her screams.

Her goddamn screams.

The terror in her voice sent chills down my spine and a gross ripple through my blood. I rushed forward, shouting her name. I called to her over and over and willed my legs to carry me faster than they were. It fell quiet quickly. Dead quiet. I called out for her again and, still, nothing.

My name was shouted from somewhere behind me, then I was hit, tackled to the ground. Air was knocked from my lungs as I crashed to the floor, and I lost my gun on impact. I didn't have time to recover. The asshole who jumped me pinned me on my back and straddled my hips. I tried to buck him off, but he held my wrists captive to the tiles beneath us and sneered down at me with his rat face.

"Mayor's gonna cook her," he said and laughed. "Serves the whore right, sleeping with the enemy."

Motherfucker. I shot forward, crunching my torso, and I grabbed him by his collar. I yanked him forward and slammed my fist into his face, tossing his head to the side.

"Shit!" I heard Judge swear, then the sound of crashing ceramics hitting the tiles ricocheted around the room. "Where's a frying pan when you need one?"

What? My attacker pulled free and cocked his arm back, but I grabbed his fist and held it prisoner. I hit him again, and pleasure rippled through me. All my stress, fear, and anger were the driving forces behind my strength as I punched him repeatedly, rocking him to his core. When his arms went limp at his sides and his spine curved weakly, I rolled him off me and hit him some more. I wanted to destroy him, to smash him into tiny pieces, for getting in my way, but I had my woman to save. So I left him an unconscious bleeding mess on the floor and made my way toward her—toward the casket that contained her battered body. I fought enemies as they came, one after the other, until I was cut, beaten, bruised, and bleeding worse than I'd ever been. Whatever was thrown at me, I gave it back tenfold while my men swept through the room like tornados, ripping everything apart. Bullets whipped passed me as I approached the casket with a bloodied face and a severe limp, and the chamber spewed out more heat than I could stand.

Tonight, Exeter's crematorium was deafeningly loud, crashing and bashing, but it was background noise to the thumping of my heart. I held my breath as I reached out and touched the wood. It was hot to my fingertips, and I yanked my fingers back with a hiss. *There's no way she's alive.* I shook the negative thought away, licked my lips, and rubbed my fingers to my palms then snatched the lid and pulled as hard as I could. It cracked, splintered, then snapped in half, and I tossed the piece over my shoulder, uncaring where it landed. All my attention was on her, on my severely beaten, overheated, helpless little woman.

"Christ," I whispered, moving to the head of the casket.

Strangely, the anger I accumulated since we were pulled over drained out through my shoes. None of it mattered. What mattered was getting Isabelle help. Even if it meant I had to come back for Jonathan another day, I had to get her out of here. I had to take her home.

I reached in and forced my hands underneath her fragile frame, hooking my hands around her armpits. She was hard to keep a hold of. Her body was slick with sweat and blood, and I couldn't get her to bend the way I wanted her to bend. Her head lolled back, and panic struck me. She looked...well, she looked dead. I gritted my teeth and tugged harder, desperate to get her out of the casket, but she wasn't budging. Armi approached first and slammed the butt of his rifle where the lid met the base. On the other side, Stoic rushed up and did the same. While they worked on the lower half of the lid, Modo slid in beside me to help support her torso; Judge did, too, and spared me a sympathetic glance I didn't acknowledge. With one final ram, the remaining piece of lid popped off, and Casino, Ayr, and Amani pushed in front of Armi and Stoic to lift Isabelle's lower half. She whimpered, a sound I barely heard, and hope ignited in my chest.

"Izzy?" I called to her, and her eyelids fluttered. "Izzy? Baby?"

We crouched, lowering her to the floor. Her tattered hospital robe was torn, exposing her entire left leg up to her bruised hip where Judge kept the

199

fabric pinched together in his dirty hands.

"Her feet…" Amani whispered and covered her mouth. "Creed…"

I glanced at her feet, and well, they didn't look much like feet. They were blistered, unlike anything I'd ever seen. I laid her head against the floor and stood up. I didn't know the extent of her injuries, if her neck was snapped or her spine shattered, but I knew I needed to get her to Harlei, our doctor, now. I stepped around her, moving in front of Modo, who couldn't stop staring at her feet, and I bent low to scoop her into my arms.

"I don't think so," a familiar voice snapped, and I lifted my head as Jonathan Laurent sauntered out of the shadows from behind the chamber, a handgun pointed directly at my face.

He sauntered slowly, and even though he was outnumbered, there was something smug about his gait. I cut my eyes at him and slowly straightened, leaving Blondie where she was. No one else made a move to kill Jonathan. They could, easy, but I made them promise to leave him for me. It made sense. Hell, it was fucking poetic I be the one to end it because, for once, I wasn't the villain of the story. I was the hero. He wanted me to be his daughter's destroyer, but I was her savior.

Her lover.

Her fucking everything.

"Wait for me outside," I told the crew, not looking at any of them.

They'd follow my orders, at least, everyone except Judge would. As expected, Judge remained after the others left, like a pain in my ass.

I stepped toward Jonathan, ignoring the invisible ties to my ankles that pulled on me, begging me not to leave an inch of distance between Isabelle and me. Jonathan smoothed a hand down the front of his navy tie as the hand that held his weapon trembled. He wasn't a fighter; turned out, neither were the men he hired. He made a mistake turning on us. We'd have kept him fed, kept him in that big old house of his, and kept Isabelle out of harm's way, but no. He betrayed us. We told him betraying us was a death sentence, no exceptions.

"I won't let you screw this up for me," he said, his eyes wide and fearful. "I won't let you ruin everything I've worked hard for just because you want to fuck my daughter."

Judge simpered and kissed his teeth. "He already did."

Jonathan grimaced, and I smirked as I eased closer.

"They're like rabbits, the two of them," Judge added, finally lifting his damn shotgun. "Always fucking."

He adjusted his stance, and I smirked when Jonathan realized we had the upper hand. Sure, he could shoot me with his little handgun, and it'd hurt, but Judge would blow his skull to nothing with his shotgun. I shot forward and snatched Jonathan's thin wrist. He shrieked as I twisted it until it made a sick popping noise and he dropped his gun.

"Wait—"

I kicked him in the knee, and he collapsed with a mighty yelp and stared up at me with pleading eyes, eyes that looked so much like Isabelle's. Was that

how she looked at him before he hurt her? I gritted
my teeth and growled and grabbed the mayor by his
face. He struggled, and his jaw clicked as he tried to
yank his head free, but he wasn't going anywhere. I
moved my thumbs and found his eyes. He squeezed
them shut, but that wasn't going to stop me. I
pressed my thumbs into his sockets, and he
hollered, but it was nothing compared to the horrific
screams I heard coming from the casket he put
Isabelle in. To me, his screaming was a lullaby, a
peaceful melody that soothed my soul. *He was
going to burn Isabelle alive.* I gritted my teeth and
pressed harder. He scraped at my forearms, my
wrists, and my face. He clawed me, deep. I felt
chunks of my skin ripping off as he raked his nails
over me. The pain breathed life into me. I wanted
more, to torture him more…but I knew Isabelle
wouldn't want him to suffer, as much as he put her
through. I released Jonathan and he fell to his knees,
clutching his face and sobbing. Dark blood ran
between his fingers and down the back of his hands.

"You won't hurt her again," I told him. "I'll
make sure of that."

I held out my empty hand, and Judge moved
close, placing his shotgun in my grip.

"You sure you want to end it so quickly?" he
asked, not letting go of the gun. "Could always take
him back to the shed."

"Nah." I pulled the gun out of his hold and
kicked Jonathan onto his ass. "Tilt your head."

Resigned, he lifted his chin, and I stared into his
bloodied eye sockets as I placed the barrel to his
forehead. I wanted him to die here, the place he

intended to murder Isabelle. I straightened my shoulders and tightened my grip. I began to squeeze the trigger when I heard it.

A whimper.

I glanced over my shoulder at Isabelle as she stared at her father kneeling at my feet. Her face was bloodied, bruised, and twisted in pain, but her eyes were enough to give me pause. She dragged her gaze up to me and caught her lower lip between her teeth. She didn't need to have a clean, clear face for me to see she didn't want me to murder her father. If anything, she looked mortified, disgusted even, and for the first time in my life, being the way I was felt gross in my veins. I hovered my finger over the trigger. I wanted to pull it and get my revenge. If I didn't, I knew it'd keep me up for the rest of my life, an unresolved problem that'd bug me relentlessly.

I needed the closure...but I didn't want her to be afraid of me.

I needed the closure...but I needed her love more.

I was whipped enough to admit her admiration fueled me more than revenge ever would. I could live with the torment of not taking Jonathan's life if it meant keeping her.

I handed Judge the shotgun and dipped my chin. Wickedness flashed in his eyes, and he nodded his head. I didn't have to verbalize anything. He knew what I wanted. I didn't want my revenge, but who was I to take it away from someone else?

"Give me that." I flicked my head toward the sweatshirt he tied around his hips.

He did without question, and I took it to Isabelle and draped it over her. Her chest heaved, and blood trickled from her mouth. *Baby.* I cursed and lifted her into my arms, and her little whimper evolved into sobbing as I carried her out of the crematorium and climbed onto my bike. Armi and Modo helped position her in front of me, her chest to mine, her legs over my thighs. She continued to cry as I took off my cut and turned it around. I put my arms through the holes and pulled it on backwards. It held her close to me and supported her back, like a sling. Then I grabbed my handlebars and eased out of the parking lot. Minutes into the drive, she went limp, and I was flying low, desperate to get her home…

…where she belonged.

* * *

At the clubhouse, Harlei and her mom, Pearl, were on standby to receive Isabelle. Within ten minutes of me arriving, they had Isabelle stripped naked and hooked up to different machines, different drips. It was overwhelming. They rushed around the room, like Izzy's life depended on it, talking gibberish. I couldn't keep up. All I did was watch the numbers on Isabelle's machines climb high and sporadically dip low with every breath she took. With every inhale, the machine beeped and told us she wasn't taking in enough air, but Harlei didn't seem worried. She said she had more important things to worry about, things that directly impacted whether Isabelle would make it or not. So

I tried not to worry about it, but it was distracting. Every beep, every ring, had my heart clenching in my chest. If she died, I was going to regret not pulling Jonathan apart.

A pointy mass hit me in the stomach, and I grunted and stepped back from the bed.

"You're too big," Harlei grumbled, elbowing me out of the way so Pearl could stick a needle and a tube in Isabelle's slender arm. "Get out of here."

"I'm not going anywhere."

"Then do something useful," she ordered, pulling open the drawers on a stainless-steel cart. She reached inside and dragged out a clear bag of liquid and a syringe with a strange plastic tip. "Flush her wounds so I can see which ones need stitching. Mom, grab the peroxide."

"What about her feet?" I demanded.

I noticed some of the blisters had ruptured and were bleeding.

"Only got two hands, Creed. I'll get to her feet when I can."

I flicked my stare over Isabelle's body. She was naked on the bed, her hospital gown completely open. Horrific bruises spotted her body and made mine ache all over. A light layer of smoke and ash covered her from head to toe, and it was hard to tell what was dirt and what was blood.

I swallowed hard and filled my first syringe with saline. I gently squeezed, and the saline squirted out the tip and cleaned her body, revealing scratches and cuts. By her ribs, a thick line of ash and blood gathered, and it took a syringe and a half to clean it out. Fresh blood seeped out when the debris was cleared, and I crouched lower to get a better look. Inside, more debris was caught, so I held the tip to the slice and I emptied the syringe, flushing it out. When the last drop hit the wound, a shadow fell over me as Harlei put her head beside mine to get a closer look.

"Shit," she swore. "Didn't see that."

"Knife wound?" I asked, my blood simmering.

"Possibly." She straightened and turned to her mother. "We don't have a thoracostomy tube. Get me an occlusive bandage and call Grant."

Pearl nodded and rushed off. I frowned. Grant was a surgeon who owed us after we helped his son out of a tough spot years ago. We were still dealing with the repercussions of attacking the Ventillis in Las Vegas. We didn't call Grant often, only when shit got serious.

Grant arrived seventeen minutes later, all scrubbed up in navy. He didn't greet me. He just went to work on Blondie, and I let him go, unbothered. I stood there for hours, holding an extra bag of…whatever it was. The sun was up and the rest of the men had returned by the time Grant was done. When he was done, he left immediately while Harlei slept against the far wall, her hands clean, but her shirt was spattered with blood. In the past, Harlei and I frequently butted heads. I even demanded Judge get rid of her more times than I could count, but in this moment, I was thankful for her. She shot around this room for hours, trying to save someone she didn't know, someone who didn't have any ties to the club. For that, she had my respect.

I watched the last of the liquid in the bag I was holding drain down the tube and into Blondie's arm. *Thank fuck.* My back hurt and the muscles in my arm screamed from holding it up, but I didn't mind it. It was the least I could do. Isabelle was clean, thanks to Pearl, and draped in a light blue gown. Her hair still held remnants of her awful time, but I'd wash it for her as soon as I could.

When her blood started to travel back up the empty tube, I pulled it out and bandaged her up, like Harlei instructed. Then I pulled up a chair and sat by her bed. My eyelids grew heavy, my limbs felt like bricks, but I couldn't drift off. There was a shitstorm coming, and I had to protect her from the fallout. But how? I kept my attention on her. I watched her eyelids flutter and her chest rise and fall with sluggish, painful-looking breaths. I wished I could switch out with her, to give her my breaths, and it was an odd feeling for me. Confusion invaded my mind. Was I in love? I didn't know. Didn't even know what it felt like to be loved. I didn't chase friendships or romance. I preferred to chase the road, to chase danger and money…until that night in Isabelle's room. From then, she was always a lingering thought in my mind. I knew I cared for her, knew I'd do anything for her, and I knew I couldn't love her alone. I needed my men to love her, too; she'd be safe then.

I shuffled on the chair and let my eyes fall shut, moving low so I could rest my head on the back rest. Sleep hit me at once, kind of like the realization I had about my feelings for Izzy, and I dreamed of her. I always dreamed of her.

SEVENTEEN

CREED

Two months had passed since the night we pulled Isabelle from the casket at the crematorium. She was healing nicely, if not fully healed. At least, that's what Harlei told me. I swallowed a mouthful of my beer and stared into the bonfire, watching the flames as they devoured the large wooden logs Modo fed to them. Truth be told, I hadn't spoken to Blondie much since that night.

She avoided all of us…

Most of them didn't notice, but I did. Every day dragged on longer than it should, and nights were colder spent on a couch or outside my room where she slept in my bed. It took every sliver of patience I had not to confront her and demand she acknowledge me or demand her to love me.

It killed me to give her space since my feelings for her only got worse and we'd barely exchanged a sentence. I wanted to hold her, to squeeze her until she popped and kiss her until my lips hurt, but she was closed off and cold. She kept me at arm's length, and I didn't know why. If it wasn't for Iris, Isabelle wouldn't eat or leave my room.

A week after that fiasco, we escorted her to Chelsea's funeral. It was a solemn thirty-motorcycle cortège. Isabelle was still recovering from her injuries, so Kace drove her in Armi's truck. We waited on the sidelines while Isabelle attended the ceremony. No one paid her any attention, even when she was sobbing as they lowered Chelsea's casket into the ground, and it hurt my fucking heart, but what could I do? At that point, I didn't exist. Only her grief did.

There hadn't been a funeral for Jonathan. As far as anyone knew, he was still missing.

The men roared with laughter, enjoying their time around the fire. It'd been a while since we were able to laugh. Following the disappearance of Jonathan, we'd been under scrutiny from the FBI. These days, they seemed to be on the lot more than we were. God knew they'd spoken to Blondie more than me. I was nervous after the first few interviews they had with her. I thought she'd throw us all to the wolves, but she didn't. She spoke her truth, explained what her father did, and maintained her innocence in his disappearance. We all told the FBI we didn't know where Jonathan went after we rescued Isabelle from the crematorium. I was the only one who knew Judge murdered Jonathan, burned him, and scattered his ashes over the hot sands of Nevada somewhere. I'd take that information to the grave.

As for the *business* side of things...while the

dust was still settling and the feds were sniffing around, business was at a standstill. We were low on money and on morale, but it was only short term, and we had to stick it out.

"He wouldn't fucking pay me," Modo boomed, spilling his can of beer.

Ayr snickered and shifted his leg, moving out of the splash zone. I simpered, entertained by Modo's story. Though we kept a low profile, some of our lesser members still did runs. I envied them. Going on runs would give me something to do. Instead, I hung around the clubhouse, doing nothing. I lifted my drink and took another mouthful when I saw a flash of pink out of the corner of my eye. No one wore pink here. No one except Blondie. I turned my head, and the sight of her strolling toward us took my breath away. The setting sun hit her milky skin and bounced off her long, blonde locks. It was cool out, but she didn't seem to care. She threaded her fingers in front of her thighs and flicked her nervous stare over our group of twelve.

As she closed the distance, I shifted in my seat and averted my attention to the bonfire. Isabelle wouldn't be coming here for me. Since Iris sat three seats to my right, I was prepared for her to walk right on by. What I wasn't prepared for was her shadow to darken my spot.

"She's looking at you, VP," Casino shouted.

Fuck. I dragged my stare from her scarred and bare feet, up her slender legs to the hem of her flowy pink dress that swayed around her knees. Most of her cuts were no longer visible, but Harlei said her feet would forever carry the heavy scarring of her father's betrayal. I inhaled through my nose and lifted my gaze to her face. Our eyes locked. Her irises were as striking as ever, and there was a warmth to them I hadn't seen in months. *God.* I missed her. More than anything. Everything about the woman who stood in front of me was utter perfection. From the highlight on her top lip to the way the wind blew strands of her hair into her pretty face. Everyone in this circle knew Isabelle Laurent turned me to putty, and they all eyed us immaturely.

I sat back in my chair and watched her. What did she want? Izzy glanced at my lap then back to my face. She wanted to sit? I moved my arms out of the way, and she turned and lowered herself onto me. I peered awkwardly at Judge, who smiled and finished off the remnants of his beer with a single swallow. What the hell was I supposed to do? We'd barely spoken to each other in months, and now she was sitting in my lap? Were we good? Was that what this meant? To test it, I placed my hand on her thigh, and it was bare and smooth where her dress lifted. Isabelle relaxed under my touch, melting against me. My dick twitched as heat gathered at the collar of my tee. I'd gone so long without her…if she made any sudden movements, I was done for.

"Anyway," Modo continued, his British accent thick. I forced my attention from Izzy's slender shoulders to his ugly face, which softened my hardening cock. "Where was I?"

"He didn't want to pay you," Ayr answered and leaned forward onto his elbows.

"Oh, right. The fucker didn't want to pay me."

"So what'd you do?" Ayr encouraged him, his

face splitting with a wide grin.

Modo flicked his gaze to Blondie then Judge. "She's one of us, isn't she? Creed's old lady?"

Isabelle straightened as Judge looked at her. He arched an eyebrow, asking her a silent question, giving her a way out. I held my breath. If she said no, she could walk away, and there wouldn't be a thing I could do to stop it. If she said yes, she was mine, and there was no walking away from this. Isabelle glanced at me over her shoulder, but I didn't make eye contact with her. I didn't want to plant the answer in her head with my expression. I wanted her to do what *she* wanted.

"Yes," she said. Her voice wrapped around my soul and squeezed tight. "I am."

For whatever reason, I looked to Judge, whose eyes flared wickedly, the dirty bastard. He was smug and satisfied because he knew her answer meant he'd get her, too.

"I tied him down," Modo said, swiping a hand down his copper beard. "And I shot him."

Ayr laughed, tossing his empty can of beer into the makeshift cardboard bin. "Tell 'em where."

"I aimed at his knee and as I pulled the trigger…" Delight danced in Modo's amber eyes. "I sneezed and shot him in the nuts."

Izzy gasped, and I laughed, squeezing her thigh. The men howled with laughter, too, and from there, the conversation separated into smaller ones. The only people not engaged in convo was Isabelle and me. She noticed, too, and twisted on my lap, awakening every cell in my body. I flicked my stare over her face, forgetting how beautiful she was, even up close.

"I miss you," she whispered, and her admission punched me in the chest.

So many weeks had passed, and it never crossed my mind that *she* missed *me*.

"I miss you, too," I said without hesitation.

My stomach turned at the heavy feeling of being vulnerable, but I couldn't help it. I wanted her to know I missed her, that I wanted to be close to her. I craved to hold her, touch her, kiss her. More than anything, I desperately desired to hold a conversation, to hear her voice in my ears. Her silence and avoidance fucking hurt, more than any wound I'd ever suffered. And I hated it. I hated I felt that way—hated that I cared so much for her—because it made me weaker.

Isabelle leaned closer and touched my cheeks. I hadn't shaved in a while, but I could still feel the softness of her hands and the warmth radiating from her palms. Her eyes flickered to my lips and back.

"Do you hate me?" she asked, leaning in until her chest touched mine. "It's okay if you do…"

Worry swam in the pools of her blue eyes and made my heartbeat through my chest. The smell of her, leather and lavender, wafted through my nose, and I forgot where I was. No one else existed. I only saw her and the flames that danced behind her.

"I hate a lot of things," I told her. "But not you. I could never hate you."

Izzy closed the distance between our lips and kissed me tenderly, until little sparks of static danced over my skin. When she finally broke the kiss, I was dazed, and her lips were swollen. Our breath eagerly clashed, our grip on each other significantly tighter than it was when we started.

"Can we go?"

I threw my unfinished can of beer to the floor and grabbed her as I stood up. She cursed as I took her whole weight in my arms, and she yelped as I put her over my shoulder.

"Don't bother me until tomorrow," I called to everyone, smoothing my hand over Izzy's backside.

They hollered, shouted, and booed, but I couldn't hear them over the pounding excitement in my ears. I made a beeline for the clubhouse, spurred on by Isabelle's laughter.

Once inside, I pulled Isabelle from my shoulder, and she wrapped her legs around my waist. We kissed, hungrily, and I was thankful I knew the layout of the club like the back of my hand. In my room, I lowered Izzy to her feet, and we continued to kiss while we yanked off pieces of each other's clothing and tossed them away. I hated the way my head spun from all the beers I drank, and I shook my head, willing the sensation to go away. I wanted to be in the moment. I wanted to be focused. I was hyperaware of the way she touched me, and I searched for any kind of hesitation in it, any hint that I was going too hard, but she reciprocated, squeezed me as hard as I squeezed her. So I didn't stop. I was relentless. I was desperate to feel every inch of her, desperate to get her out of her lingerie. She cupped my face as I plunged my tongue inside her mouth and gripped the hem of her black lace panties. I tugged, ripping the seam, and she gasped as the fabric gave away on the left side of her hip. I moved to the right side and caught the lacy fabric between my fingers as Izzy planted her hands on my chest. The back of my calves hit the leather, and she broke the kiss.

"I want to taste you," she panted then shoved me onto the couch.

I fell and was caught by the leather. I stared up at her, at her disheveled hair as strands whirled around her face, and at her eyes, which were a wild blue. Fuck that. I wanted to be inside her. *Now.* I gripped her wrists and pulled her onto me.

"Later," I said as she straddled my hips and pressed her breasts to my chest. It drove me crazy. "I need to feel you on me."

I swallowed the distance between us and shoved my tongue in her mouth. While I kissed her, I moved her tattered panties to the side, and she maneuvered her hips and took my cock out of my unbuttoned jeans. The zipper bit into the base of my shaft, but I didn't care. I was too distracted by the way she was taking control, by the way she flexed her hips and slipped her soft, wet, and warm entrance over my tip and took me inside her. I shivered and groaned. It felt like a lifetime ago that I was with her like this. She was perfection. My perfection.

Isabelle moaned into my mouth, kissing me harder. I flexed my hips, wanting to get deeper, to feel more of her. When I was as deep as I possibly could be, she peeled her lips from mine and tilted her head back with a moan. I squeezed her ass in my hands and licked the column of her throat as she grinded on me. She felt good. She always felt good.

I gritted my teeth against the pressure building between my legs. There was nowhere for me to go to get away from the pleasure she was giving me.

I broke the kiss and clamped down on her ass, imprisoning her in my grip. "Christ, Iz."

For the first time in my life, I'd reached my peak in an embarrassingly short amount of time. It was a testament to how bad she turned me on. Sensing it, Isabelle stopped moving and cupped my face in her warm palms. I stared into the glistening pools of her eyes, and she flicked her thumbs over my cheekbones. I knew in that moment, as she stared at me so affectionately, that I'd do anything for her. Izzy was the metal to my magnet, the bright sun in my dark universe, and I knew—without a doubt— I'd fallen in love with her.

IZZY

I cup his handsome face in my hands and admire the way the setting sunlight pours in through the window and surrounds his head, like a halo. Though James Creed wears the devil's name on his back, I'm convinced he's an angel. In fact, his tummy-tightening smirk is the only thing I find devilish about him.

He's been infinitely patient with me over the past two months. I've avoided him like the plague because I needed to heal mentally, and physically, before coming face to face with him. I needed to make sure I was able to talk to Creed without spiraling back to that night. The first few weeks, all I could think about was his large thumbs buried inside my father's eye sockets. I've never witnessed such violence, but Judge helped me process it. He showed me how to focus on the fact I'd be dead if it weren't for Creed and that the violence was a necessary evil. Judge also told me he was the one who ended my father and that Creed's aggression was nothing compared to what he did. I swallow the urge to shudder. Creed is scary, but Judge is something else entirely.

Mostly, I drown in the grief of losing my best friend so horrifically. I couldn't save her. I…I didn't even try. I was so consumed by revenge, by the idea of outing my father on live television, I didn't consider that my actions would condemn her to such a violent death. I thought my father was bluffing, and I'll never forgive myself for it.

All things considered, I'm in a good place today. I don't ever want to discuss what happened. I just want to put it behind me and move forward with the man who saved my life and has provided for me these past few months. Without him, where would I be?

I'm pulled from my thoughts by Creed's index finger as he gently glides it along my lower lip. He locks me in his dark, whiskey gaze, and my stomach tightens. I squeeze him between my thighs, and although we aren't moving, he remains rock hard inside me.

"I was scared," he says, an embarrassed look crossing his features. "That that was gonna lose you…that I was losing you."

"You saved me," I murmur. "I'm not going anywhere. You're all I have now."

Creed swallows hard.

"Do you love me?" he asks, brushing his nose against mine.

My eyebrows lift of their own accord. Do I love him? Do I love the man who fought for me? Who saved my life? As far as I know, I'm the only Laurent from our family tree there is left. My parents have no siblings, and both their parents have long since passed. Chelsea is gone, and I don't care where Pierce is or what he's doing. All I have is Creed and the mischievous band of weirdos that'll follow him to the end of the world, and that's more than enough.

"Yes." I touch his hair, pushing my fingers through it to massage his scalp. "Do you love me?"

I hold my breath until my lungs begin to burn. I didn't realize how bad I want him to love me—how bad I *need* him to love me.

Creed's irises turn lively, their honey rivers sparkling. "Yeah."

Then he crushes his mouth to mine and kisses me in a way only he can. I open my mouth to him, and his tongue is right there, moving against mine, as he releases a husky groan of pleasure. I love the masculine sound of him and the giant buzz of energy he sends through my veins.

Creed smooths his palms over my backside and moves to my thighs. He pushes me then digs his fingers into my flesh and pulls me back, making me grind against him. Heat blooms over my body, and I take the lead, rolling against him while I push my tongue into his mouth. I know he's dangerously close to spilling over, that he's holding on for my sake, but I don't need him to. I slow my kiss and pay attention to my tongue as I move it at a languid pace against his. Creed's groans surround me—his cursing and swearing, too—and my name is a shot of pure arousal on the tip of his tongue, making the skin on the back of my neck vibrate deliciously. Breaking the kiss, he lowers his forehead to my collar bone and groans again. He tightens his grip to a bruising pressure, and I feel him spill and pulse inside me as his heavy breathing turns uneven and quick. I'm held still, imprisoned in his grip, and we remain like that well after he softens and his breathing returns to normal. Afterward, he lowers me to the couch, and we lay chest to chest, our legs a tangled mess, our mouths only inches apart.

He's gentle and caring, dancing the rough tips of his fingers up and down my side, eliciting goosebumps. He treks his touch everywhere, down to my thighs, my calves, and the sides of my feet. His touch is muted there by the heavy scarring, and insecurity eats away at me, like acid on rope.

"Did you see my feet?" I ask, pressing my fingertip to his throat to caress his Adam's apple.

Sympathy flashes through his eyes. "Yes."

"They're ugly."

"Ugly? They're not ugly." He frowns in thought. "You want me to kiss 'em?"

"What?" I laugh and snuggle closer. "No. I don't want you to kiss them."

"They're not ugly. Nothing about you is ugly."

Warmth flows through me, and he kisses me tenderly on my lips, gentle pecks filled with genuine adoration. Dazed, I lose myself in his beautiful amber irises and am lulled by his wildly beating heart as it thumps into mine. I want to stay like this forever. It's warm here. It feels good here with my man, the one I was never meant to have.

"I'll get you your own cut," he says, brushing my hair away from my back. "It'll have my name on it."

I can't wait to be his officially. I can't wait to be a part of the club. "Does it come in pink?"

He snorts and smiles, exposing his white, straight teeth. "Not likely."

I snuggle in closer to him, nestling into the crook of his neck, and we stay that way until the sun's final rays disappear and the high moon is shining through the skylight above his bed. The men outside have long since moved inside. Music thumps, shouting ensues, and I can't help the happy curve to my lips. This is home.

Home has never felt so wonderful and lively.

"I'll look after you," Creed whispers in my ear. "You're my old lady now."

I smile and close my eyes, committing this moment to memory and vowing never to let it fade.

EPILOGUE

IZZY

Two years later

I'm not nervous. I mentally prepared myself for this night a long time ago.

The sight of Judge and Creed sitting side by side on our new, dark leather couch wearing nothing but black sweatpants has my heart racing. Even in the dim, moody lighting, they look good. They look *really* good. Their skin is inked and smooth, and their muscular compositions are almost identical to one another. They both watch me with a hunger that almost makes me regret teasing them all dinner. *Almost.*

I lift myself from my ass to rest on my heels and grab my wine glass off the coffee table. I drink the last mouthful and place it back down, licking my lips.

Over the years, Creed has made sure Damon and I shared little, non-physical moments to make this one big moment easier for me. He expertly built the tension between us, and although I can't wait to get my hands on Judge once and for all, tonight is more than unorthodox sex. Tonight ensures I'm a part of the club. It ensures I'll be taken care of for the rest of my life, should anything happen to Creed.

"Come sit here," Creed says, his eyes flashing dangerously.

I flick my chin to the tiny space between him and Judge. "Between you?"

If I sit there, I'll be touching them both. Heat blooms down my spine at the thought. I'm not dressed for the night they seem to have planned. Though I'm braless underneath my cropped, pink tee that reads "when God made man she was only joking," a baggy pair of gray sweatpants cover my freshly waxed legs. When Creed and I spoke of this event, we discussed me wearing a naughty, black babydoll, not sweatpants.

Creed hums. "Be a good girl, like we practiced, and between us is how you'll spend the rest of your night."

More heat flushes through me. I spare a nervous glance at the pump bottle of lube next to my bottle of red wine and take a deep breath. *God. I hope Judge isn't bigger than James or any of the toys I have.*

I lift myself to my feet and saunter toward them. They watch me, closely, their large hands resting on their thighs. Judge drums his fingers, tapping in a way that intimidates me. I can please Creed like it's second nature, but Judge? I think back to that night in his room, the night I first went to the clubhouse and they were having a party. I ended up in his room by mistake, and his touch was brutal and ruthless, to say the least. *Creed still doesn't know about that...*

I turn my attention to Judge, and his charcoal eyes flash, reminding me of lightning at the peak of a summer storm. I lower myself into the space between them, flushing when my shoulders press firmly to theirs.

"Go on," Creed says, and I turn my head to look at him. He's watching Judge, his features firm. "You said her tits were turning you on."

Oh. I lift my eyebrows as a fierce blush rushes up my neck and pours into my cheeks. *He said that? To Creed?* I swallow as Judge lifts my cropped tee, bunching the fabric above my breasts. I glance at his face then down at my mounds of flesh. My nipples harden instantly, and Judge drags his finger underneath one, sending a spiral of sensation down my spine. Surprised, I place my hand on Creed's thigh and clench it as Judge cups my left breast in his large hand. My cup size is on the larger side, but in Judge's hands, much like Creed's, they feel so much smaller. He lifts it, feels the weight of it, and gently squeezes it. Without thought, I angle my torso in his direction, drawn in by lust and curiosity, and his wicked dark eyes flick to mine.

"Bigger nipples than I expected, Blondie," he says, laughter in his voice. "They're fucking perfect."

Creed hums his agreement. I straighten my spine as Judge cranes his neck and envelops my nipple and a good portion of my breast into his mouth. I suck air between my teeth and pull back, resting against Creed, who's turned with me and catches me against his chest. Creed smooths his hands along my bare waist and tugs me, moving my whole body to face Judge, who leans over me, mouthing my breasts with more need than I ever thought he could exhibit. *He really wants it.* I don't know why that surprises me.

Judge sucks me hard, desperately, while he palms my other breast, then sensually tongues it, as if it's my mouth he's kissing. When he finally breaks his hold, my nipple feels swollen and hot, and I make a disappointed sound in my throat, earning a simper from both men.

"I think she liked that," Creed says, brushing locks of my wild blonde hair from my chest.

I turn my head to look at Creed, who peers down at me, his eyes lusty and hooded. That's when I feel his hard length against my spine.

"Relax," he whispers and cranes his neck to lick my bottom lip, making my breath hitch.

"You're not jealous?"

"I'm extremely fucking jealous, but your enjoyment is the only thing appeasing me, so," he places one of my hands on my breast, the other on Judge's head, who licks at my tense abdomen, "save me from committing murder by enjoying the shit out of it."

Judge trails his thick fingers down my stomach, and I clench as he reaches the waistband of my sweatpants—the point of no return. He hooks his fingers around it, and I hold my breath as he rears back, pulling my pants down, leaving me in my lacy, white underwear. A warm flush sweeps up my spine and engulfs my neck under his gaze.

"What else does she like?" he asks, his voice thick and raspy.

"Anything. Everything." Creed cups my right breast in his hand and tweaks my nipple the way I like it. I sigh and arch my back, pushing further into his touch. "You're not hard to please, are you, Blondie?"

I shake my head. "No."

Judge keeps his eyes on mine as he glides his palm along my calf to the inside of my knee. He lays himself on his stomach and brings his face dangerously close to my clothed core. Without a word, he pushes my leg up and away, opening me up to him. Creed releases my nipple, and I relax against him as he replaces Judge's hold under my knee.

"Lick her thighs," Creed tells him. "She likes that."

Simpering, Judge licks his lower lip then drags his tongue up my inner thigh, licking his way to the apex. As he goes, Creed kisses me behind the ear and down my neck, making me shiver. I revel in the sensation as he sweeps my hair out of the way and trails his nose along my heated flesh, breathing me in. I close my eyes. I've imagined this night in my head for a long time, fantasized about it, but I didn't imagine it feeling this seamless. Two different men doing two different things to me at the same time is almost overwhelming.

Fingers brush against my lace-covered entrance, and I jolt, my eyes shooting open. Underneath me,

Creed's body tightens.

"Pull her panties to the side," he orders, and Judge obliges.

My lips part as his warm breath blows against my wet, exposed flesh, and Creed's chest rises and falls quicker, his breath blowing faster against the shell of my ear, heating me up beyond belief.

"He must really like you," Creed whispers. "He doesn't eat pussy. Ever."

"Ever?"

He bites my neck, and I flex my hips, my pussy grazing Judge's full lips. "Ever."

Judge buries his face between my legs and pushes his tongue between my creases. My hands fly to his head as I quiver, and I suck air between my teeth, digging my nails into his scalp.

"Judge…" I say, breathless, a plea for…*something*. I don't know what. "Fuck."

He groans heartily, sending a hot surge of pleasure rolling through my stomach, then ravenously devours me, tonguing, kissing, and mouthing his way around my clit the way I like it, the way Creed does it too, and the way Pierce rarely got right.

It surprises me Judge doesn't do this. If he doesn't like it, then he's good at pretending.

Creed snatches my breasts in his hands and kneads them, rolling my hardened peaks between his fingers, taking me higher and higher. I moan loudly, making Creed curse and squirm underneath me. I pull my right hand from Judge's head and lift my arm to clasp the back of Creed's neck. I pull on it, wanting more, wanting Creed on me, too. Judge lashes me with his tongue, and I'm suddenly loud. My cries ring in my ears, and my calves and thighs tremble as he works me up with his mouth. Then he glides the back of his hand along my inner thigh, toward my heat. Without breaking contact with his tongue, he presses two fingers to my opening then slips them inside me. I arch my back, grinding my hips into his mouth as sensations explode at the base of my spine.

"Should I make him to stop?" Creed asks, and I can hear the teasing tone in his deep, raspy tenor.

"No," I beg, digging my fingernails into the skin on the back of his neck. He'd make Judge stop, just to toy with me. "Please let him keep going."

"You want him to make you come?"

I nod, rapidly moving my hips quicker, seeking my orgasm before it's taken away. Creed releases a guttural groan from his chest and pulls on my knee, opening me wider. I curse, and it doesn't take long for my orgasm to surface and bubble in the pit of my belly, waiting to spill over.

"She likes your mouth," Creed tells Judge, approval dripping from his tone. "She likes the way you fuck her with your fingers. How does she taste?"

Judge groans and releases my sensitive bundle of nerves. "Fucking good. Better than good."

He returns to pleasuring me, and it doesn't take long for my orgasm to rebuild. I squeeze my eyes shut as unbearable tingles spread like wildfire over my body, setting fire to every nerve, every cell, in my being. Judge's name is quick and sexy on the tip of my tongue as I grind my pelvis into his face, and the pleasure he stirs in me overrides my system. In seconds, my body is awash in ecstasy as my orgasm crashes over me. I ride it out until my bones feel like jelly and my muscles are too heavy to hold up. I rest against Creed, lost in my fog, as Judge kisses and licks at my thighs. They talk to each other, but I'm not paying attention, until I'm lifted into Judge's arms and flipped, laying chest to chest with Creed. Against him is where I want to be the most. I want James in front of me, my eyes on him and only him. *Does he know that?* I lift my eyebrows, silently asking him, and I shift, moving further up his wide body so our noses kiss. His answer comes in the form of a hot, possessive kiss. He knows, without a doubt, that I am his and he is mine. I push my fingers through his freshly cut hair and rest my elbows in the space above his massive shoulders. Suddenly, I wish the room wasn't so dimly lit so I could see the rivers of honey in his eyes and the ochre highlights in his dark, freshly cut hair. A few feet behind us, the sounds of glass tinkering tells me Judge is pouring himself another drink.

"Your turn," I say to Creed, flicking my tongue over his lower lip. "Make me feel good?"

Amusement flashes in his eyes. "You're being greedy."

I smirk and nod because I know I am. Judge holds two rocks glasses of whiskey beside us, and we take it without thanks, downing our mouthful.

"I think it's your turn," Creed says. "I want you to suck me while he watches."

A whoosh of tingles rushes over me, and I descend on his body, kissing and licking every rise and depression of his perfectly sculpted torso. He's lost weight in the time we've been together. He's leaner, his muscles more cut, and I love to lick their crevices, to rub my body against them.

When I reach the waistband of his sweatpants, I pull the front of his pants down, and his impressive length springs free. I keep my eyes on his as I lick his thick, long shaft from bottom to top then draw him into my mouth, sucking him deep.

"Damon," Creed calls. "Her underwear. Get rid of them."

The sound of a glass being set down on the coffee table tinkles in the warm, silent room. A few heartbeats pass before I feel his fingers against my left hip then a rough tug. Fabric snaps, and he repeats it on the other side. After Judge has ripped my panties from my body, he palms my ass and lifts me higher so I'm on display for him. He opens and closes my cheeks and my pussy lips, inspecting me with his eager hands. Initially, I thought it'd be hard to control Judge. As president of the MC and Creed's superior, I was worried he'd take the role as alpha, but he's doing a good job respecting me and not stepping on Creed's toes.

"Feel how wet she gets when I'm buried in her throat."

I flex my hips as Judge presses his fingers into my creases then probes inside me. I moan against Creed's hot shaft as lust shoots down my spine and shakes me to my core. Creed pushes deeper, until I gag, then he holds me there. My eyes water, and I can't breathe, but he doesn't care. He forces me to adjust to the depth, and I do. I always do.

Judge makes a comment about fucking me. My heart pounds so loud in my ears that I miss the second half of it, but I don't miss the feel of his hot flesh as it slaps against my pulsing, wet core. I shiver, bobbing my head high enough to breathe through my nose. Judge presses the large head of his cock to my entrance and applies pressure, stretching me. I gasp, pulling off Creed's dick.

"Don't you fucking dare put it in," Creed snaps at him. "I told you her pussy is mine."

"Creed," Judge groans and painfully squeezes one of my ass cheeks in one hand while jerking himself against me, rubbing the head of his cock against my clit. "You're a fucking asshole."

Creed smirks. I think he enjoys toying with Judge. I grab Creed by his shaft and work him in my hand, making his hips flex and his abs clench. His hungry stare flicks between my bouncy breasts and my face, and as I pump him, Judge continues to rub himself against my sensitive bundle of nerves, bringing me closer and closer to my second orgasm. He must know it too because the sneaky asshole pushes against my entrance again, this time his whole head enters me, and I pull away with a gasp as Creed's previous demand flutters to the forefront of my mind. Ashamedly, I wish he'd plunge in and fuck me against Creed until I came.

"I want to feel it," Judge groans, his breathing quick, his tone tormented. "I want to feel her come around my cock."

Creed cups my face in his hands and crunches his body, bringing his mouth closer to mine. "Is that what you want, baby? You want his cock inside you?"

I've never lied to him. Right now, I've got two sexy men in my sitting room with their cocks out, and I'm filled to the brim with lust. It's a no brainer.

"Yes," I utter, easing back against Judge, who keeps the head of his length at bay. "Please."

Creed flicks his stare to Judge then back to me. Whatever passes between them, Judge takes it as permission. He grips my hips and slams inside me with a guttural groan. I hiss and grit my teeth as he fills me completely and hits my cervix. For stability, I grip Creed as hard as I can.

"Rub me," I tell him, pulling on his forearm with my free hand while I continue to stroke him with the other. "*Please*, James."

He reaches between my legs places his rough fingers against my clit and rubs me hard while Judge strikes fast and deep. In seconds, I completely shatter apart, coming harder than I think I ever have. The aftershocks barely wear off when I'm pulled off Judge and I'm back on Creed, straddling his hip, his own cock hard against my ass, between my firm, round cheeks. He pushes my hair out of my face then grips my ass and lifts me so his length rests between us.

"Are you ready for me?" he asks, and I lick my lips and smirk at him.

"Yeah, baby," I say, breathless. "I'm ready for you."

He eases inside, and I close my eyes as he squeezes his way in, swearing under his breath. He's thicker than Judge but more familiar, and my body welcomes him immediately, making it wet and stretchy enough to fit him. To help it along, I gently lift and lower myself and crane my neck to kiss him on the mouth. It's the only hard limit I've set with Judge. I don't want to kiss him, only my man.

Cold liquid hits my backside, and I squeak, breaking the kiss. Creed shushes me and hooks my chin with his finger, bringing my mouth back to his. Then I feel a finger there, at my back entrance, and I tighten, focusing more on that than the feel of Creed's tongue in my mouth.

Judge gently pushes inside, and I gasp, groaning at the intrusion, at the full feeling that sweeps over me at the prod of his finger. I'm not scared. I've prepared for this act. Creed made sure of it. Judge adds another finger and squirts more lube until he's able to move them with ease, and the feeling his ministrations elicit makes me crave more.

Kissing me deeply, Creed retreats from my body along with Judge's fingers, and behind me, I hear the ripping of a condom wrapper then more lube squirting. Judge comes back on a different angle and presses the head of his hard cock against me. I break the kiss one more time and turn my head, only to be caught by Creed's large hands as he cups my face and presses my nose to his. I breathe quickly against his lips, and a light sweat blooms over my body. *Maybe I'm a little scared.* Judge pushes deeper, and I feel my tightest passage stretch. I cringe, my lips parting to let out a rush of air, and I cling to Creed, as if burying my nails in his flesh will ease the burning. *Fuck.* Creed plants gentle kisses all over my lips and whispers for me to relax, but I can't relax. I'm in my head too much. I feel full already. How the hell am I supposed to have them both? Releasing my face, Creed glides his large, rough hands down my sides to my ass. I feel Judge rear back behind me, leaving the very tip of himself inside.

"It's easy," Creed tells me, his irises darkening, his lids growing heavier. "You just gotta let him in."

He pushes on me, easing me back against Judge, who remains steadfast and strong, like a concrete pillar, and I inhale through my nose. Creed's push slips Judge deeper, and I exhale as he pulls me back, lessening the amount of tension deep within me. He hums his encouragement then pushes me again, harder this time, and Judge swears as I take him deeper. More cold, soothing liquid hits my heated flesh, and Creed pushes and pulls me quicker, more frequently, moving me up and down his friend's thickening length. When I've adjusted, when my tension has mostly dissipated, Creed pushes his way inside my body, and I feel...I just feel so full.

When both men are fully inside me, neither insist on thrusting. Instead, they rub me, their hot, damp hands massaging my muscles, their mouths skimming my flesh, their tongues tasting, and their teeth biting. In the span of an hour, they fulfill every fantasy I've ever had about having multiple men at the same time, but I don't think I'd do it again. It's a strange phenomenon...Creed is as close as he can possibly be—he's literally inside my body—but I've never felt so far away from him. While Judge makes my stomach flutter, it's Creed who makes my soul sing.

Our breaths heat and quicken, all three of us, and the sensation of having two cocks inside of me, both throbbing and pumping at alternate times, moving like a well-oiled machine, is overwhelming. It dawns on me then that they're perfectly rehearsed and I'm the only one here who has no idea what's going to happen next. I cut my eyes at Creed, who grips the back of my neck and squeezes, holding me as close as he possibly can.

"You've done this before," I say, matter of fact, and Judge laughs darkly as Creed's lips quirk.

"Creed loves to share his women with me."

"This is the only time it's ever meant something. Promise." Creed's eyes sparkle with amusement, his face slack with his pleasure. "And never again after tonight. You're mine. *Only* mine."

Judge thrusts hard, and I gasp as pain and pleasure dance in the pit of my belly.

"Maybe she'll get a taste for it," Judge teases, snaking his fingers through my hair and over the back of my scalp. He tugs on me, pulling my chest from Creed's and pressing my back against his. He wraps his large arms around me and rubs my body all over, touching and caressing, pinching and pulling. "Maybe she'll want this every weekend."

I shake my head and feel him smile against my ear. I close my eyes.

"Or maybe you'll want me," he adds, keeping me away from Creed. "Only me."

A thumb slides between my creases, circling my clit, and my eyes shoot open as I groan my disagreement. I could never want Judge the way I want Creed. It's been Creed from the beginning, from the moment I saw him sitting atop his bike, looking dangerous. He has eyes that make my heart beat quicker than anyone has ever made it beat and lips that send every muscle in my body coiling with desire. Judge is hot—impossibly so—but Creed is the sun my universe revolves around. I watch Creed as he rubs me, his dark eyes not leaving mine for a second.

"You'll want him?" Creed asks, and I shake my head, pressing my lips together to hold back a moan that vibrates in my throat.

"She's so hot, so tight," Judge groans, his breathing labored. He continues to thrust, moving Creed inside me also. "I think she's lying."

"I'm not lying," I snap, but my aggression quickly melts under the stroking of Creed's thumb. My head sags forward, and I can't take my eyes off the veins in his manly hands. *Perfect.* "Shit."

I move my hips, each flex controlled by the friction his tough thumb generates against my sensitive flesh. I barrel toward my climax and clasp my hand over my mouth. Creed flicks his stare over my thighs to where he fills my pussy. I pulse with need around his length, and he can feel it.

"You're gonna come on him again?" Creed says, smirking wickedly. "Maybe you do want him."

I *don't* want him. I clench Creed's thick wrist and squeeze, trying to pull him away so I don't orgasm, but my strength is no match for his. "James, s-stop it."

Creed looks at Judge and flicks his chin, gesturing for something. Smirking, Judge reaches around me and snatches my wrists, and I inhale sharply as he pulls my arms behind my back and grips me behind my elbows.

"James…" I protest pathetically, quivering as my orgasm builds and builds. "Damon…"

I grit my teeth, fighting off the pleasure that threatens to overwhelm me, but Creed isn't giving up without a fight. Creed rubs me harder, faster, and talks dirty to me. He teases me about Judge, about how needy and dirty I am. He makes me feel like a whore without letting the word leave his mouth, and I…I love it. He thrusts his hips, so does Judge, and I inhale, but I can't fill my lungs.

"Oh, fuck," I shout as I'm thrown over the edge of pleasure and left to crash into pieces on the other side. "I'm coming. I'm coming. I'm coming."

I arch my back and bite back my cry as my orgasm slams into me. It overcomes me in merciless pulses, shaking me so hard I'm certain I'd fall and shatter into a million pieces if I weren't sandwiched between the two men who force me to pulse and squirm around their lengths until I can no longer bear it.

Groaning, Judge releases me, and I collapse into Creed's arms. I tremble against him, breathing heavily through my nose, on the verge of tears as my head spins. Judge grabs my hips in his bruising grip and pounds into me five times before his hips jar and he shoves himself deep and holds still. I feel him throb inside as his release shoots into the condom.

Then it's Creed's turn. He grips my shoulders and lifts me off him, pushing me back into Judge's arms, who gratefully holds me to his torso and pulls me back a little further so Creed can see every private inch of me.

"Bounce on his cock, baby," Judge groans in my ear, his length softening inside me, making more room. "Make him come for you."

I roll my hips, but my movement is tired, and my breath is heavy. Nearly every muscle in my body feels like jelly.

"Help me," I ask Judge, lifting my arm to wrap it around his neck, pulling his head closer to mine.

Judge grabs me under my thighs and lifts me, making it easier to move myself up and down on Creed's bare, thick length. As my orgasm fades to memory, I find my strength, and Judge releases me, moving his hand to play with my hypersensitive bundle of nerves. I curse and close my eyes for a brief second. I open them as Creed grabs my calves and cranes his neck to watch me move on him. Then his grunting and groaning starts, and his lips part as he releases hot, thick ropes of his pleasure deep inside me. When he's done, Judge eases me forward, and I rest in Creed's arms once more. A few seconds pass, and they both pull out of me, leaving me empty. I release a sigh of relief I didn't realize I was holding and lick my parched lips while I listen to the sound of Creed's racing heart.

"I'm gonna have a drink, recuperate, then we can get started on round two," Judge says, moving away from the couch.

Creed tightens his hold on me, but I heard the hint of playfulness in Judge's voice. I reach out and grab the chocolate-colored throw blanket from the back of the couch and pull it over my body. In the distance, I hear the annoying squeak of the bathroom door.

"Get out," I call out then yawn. "Done with you."

"Ouch," he shouts back. "I feel used."

I lift my head to look Creed in the face and rest my chin on his chest. Smiling, he cups my face and kisses me tenderly. He keeps his tongue at bay at first then brings it into the mix, kissing me dizzy.

"You have to wash me," I tell him when he breaks the kiss.

"All right."

The blanket is lifted by my ass and cool air swoops in followed by wildfire as a bare hand slaps across my left cheek. I shriek and turn, making Creed grunt as I dig my elbow into his ribs. "What the hell, Judge?"

"Thanks for the good time, Blondie." He zips up his jacket. "Don't be late tomorrow, Creed. We have an important meeting."

"Yeah. I'll be there."

Creed rolls his large body, moving me to lay flat on the couch. He pulls his pants all the way up and adjusts the band on his hips. He turns as Judge makes his way to the front door, and I catch him by his hand, holding him back. Creed looks at me.

"Let him go. He's big enough to walk himself out."

He leans his big body over me. "Do you need me?"

I glance at his mouth. It's amazing how quickly he can rebuild my sexual need for him seconds after shattering it completely. "I need you. Only you."

I lift off the couch and kiss him. I keep kissing him until he lowers his body to mine and crushes me perfectly under his weight. I don't know how long we lay on the couch, kissing, but eventually, he's back inside me, thrusting, squeezing, pulling, pinching, rubbing. He brings me to the edge over and over until we come apart together, and I've never felt as close to him as I do now. Judge was a necessary fun to cement my life in the club, but it's Creed who steals my breath and consumes my soul.

He's the love of my life, my biker, my hero.

COMING SOON

Burning Daylight

A Devil's Cartel MC novel
Book Two

About the Author

SKYLA MADI is an Australian writer from Brisbane, Queensland.

Skyla started her writing career fresh out of high school and at 21 she is a giver of both real and fictional life.

She is an aquarian, lover of the written word and author of the #1 BESTSELLING Consumed trilogy.

Skyla LOVES to hear from readers! Here are some of ways to get into contact with her:

FACEBOOK:
https://www.facebook.com/SkylaMadi

TWITTER:
https://twitter.com/Skyla_Madi

GOODREADS
http://www.goodreads.com/author/show/6554179.Skyla_Madi

Join our Reader Group on Facebook and don't miss out on meeting our authors and entering epic giveaways!

Limitless Reading

Where reading a book
is your first step to becoming
limitless...

LIMITLESS PUBLISHING *Reader Group*

Join today! *"Where reading a book is your first step to becoming limitless..."*

https://www.facebook.com/groups/Limitless Reading/

www.ingramcontent.com/pod-product-compliance
Lightning Source LLC
Chambersburg PA
CBHW020401210626
46816CB00006BB/2076